She looked at hi[m] with uncertainty

Toni wasn't quite sure how Rafe intended saying goodbye to her. From the ironic curve of his lips he knew only too well what she was thinking.

"Let's try shaking hands," Rafe suggested. "That shouldn't cause any complications with Sean."

Her breath came out on a sigh. "Don't make fun of me, Rafe. I can't help the way I am."

"Neither can I." He paused, studying her, eyes veiled by something only he could be sure of. "So we'll start at square one again," he murmured. "Something like this."

The kiss was over quickly—too quickly. It left her yearning the way it had been intended to. Then he was gone, striding away without a backward glance; a man she hadn't even begun to understand....

KAY THORPE
is also the author of these

Harlequin Presents

and these
Harlequin Romances

Many of these titles are available at your local bookseller.

For a free catalogue listing all available Harlequin Romances
and Harlequin Presents, send your name and address to:

HARLEQUIN READER SERVICE
1440 South Priest Drive, Tempe, AZ 85281
Canadian address: Stratford, Ontario N5A 6W2

KAY THORPE

copper lake

Harlequin Books

TORONTO • LONDON • LOS ANGELES • AMSTERDAM
SYDNEY • HAMBURG • PARIS • STOCKHOLM • ATHENS • TOKYO

Harlequin Presents edition published September 1981
ISBN 0-373-10455-3

Original hardcover edition published in 1981
by Mills & Boon Limited

CHAPTER ONE

THE sudden appearance of the long white car around the bend just ahead brought Toni back to earth with a sickening jolt, tensing nerve and sinew in the horror-struck realisation that both the oncoming vehicle and her own were occupying the same lane. Even as the knowledge hit her the other driver was already reacting, swerving the car to the outside of hers with a screaming of brake linings and a smell of burning rubber.

Her own swerve was instinctive and fortunately in the opposite direction, the convertible leaving the firmer road surface to bump over rough ground for what seemed an age before finally coming to rest at an acute angle with both front wheels firmly embedded in the shallow gully which up until now had been hidden by long grass.

Face white and breath coming in shallow gasps, she leaned her head on the clenched hands still grasping the wheel and fought for control over her shattered nerves. That was the closest she had ever been to death. Bare seconds had separated both vehicles from a head-on-crash from which neither driver could have hoped to emerge. And all her fault too. She had been on the wrong side of the road—too immersed in her thoughts to register her automatic drift into the left-hand lane.

Vaguely she was aware of the slamming of a door and the sound of running footsteps, deadened as they reached the grass. Someone came up by the side of the car, and a hand reached in to touch her shoulder.

'You okay?' demanded a brusque masculine voice.

Toni pushed herself slowly into an upright position, tilting her head to look into grimly set features with a

5

sense of distortion, almost as if she were outside herself watching the scene from a distance.

'Yes,' she said. 'Yes, I'm all right, thanks.' Her voice sounded shaky; she made an effort to calm it. 'I'm sorry, it was all my fault.'

'Glad you realise it.' The brusqueness was more pronounced, one lean brown hand going up to rake back the thick dark hair from his face in a gesture which bespoke his own tension. 'If you prefer driving on the left you should have stayed in your own country.'

'It was hardly a matter of preference. I was thinking about something else and lost track of where I was, that's all.' Reaction was setting in now, her own temper rising at his tone. 'Look, I said I was sorry.'

'And that makes everything just fine?' The sarcasm grated. 'If you can't keep your mind on what you're supposed to be doing you're not fit to be on the road—*any* road!'

Green eyes sparked. 'I suppose I'm typical of all women drivers in your estimation? You strike me as just the type to harbour that kind of prejudice!'

'Wrong.' The Canadian sounded unmoved. 'I know of a great many excellent women drivers. You're one on your own.' The cool grey gaze raked over the slender length of her, resting a brief moment on the slipped top button of her white shirt before coming back to her face. 'Touring?'

Toni shrugged slim shoulders, determined to provide no further ammunition. 'I hardly think my reasons for being in British Columbia would be of any interest to you. Thanks for stopping anyway.'

'The least I could do.' He moved a step away from the car to cast an eye over it, mouth twisting. 'Not going to be easy hauling you out of there.'

'You don't have to bother trying,' she returned stiffly. 'I'll get help from the proper people.'

Dark brows lifted. 'How? There's nothing between here

and Clearview, and that's fifteen miles.'

'Someone else will pass.'

'Sure. There's always traffic on Highway One.' His lip curled. 'Don't be any dumber than you have to be. I've a tow line in the trunk. Sit tight while I get it.'

Toni did as she was told because there seemed little choice, but her pride smarted. That there was some justification in his anger, she had to concede, but did he really have to be quite so objectionable about it? Normally her driving was more than adequate to any demands made on it. It was just that she had so much on her mind at present. If she had had any sense she would have gone back home to England after leaving that job in Vancouver instead of making this trip. As the boom town of the West, Calgary was likely to offer many fine opportunities for employment, but was another job here really what she wanted? Had it not been for Randy it would never have entered her head to leave England at all.

Randy. The thought of him still had the power to hurt. How could she have been so wrong about him? Love was often called a blind emotion, and now she knew why. She had deliberately shut her eyes to all but what she had wanted to see, convinced herself that what they had was enough. But it hadn't been. Not when put to the test. Her emotions had betrayed her.

She had met him at a party, attracted on sight to the tall, fair Canadian with the clean-cut features and laughing blue eyes. The laughter had grown at her involuntary if fleeting response to his introduction. He was growing accustomed, he'd said, to the connotations his name aroused over here.

Toni had liked him all the more for his ability to take the joke against himself, and had not been at all loath to see him again. He was on a year's loan to the British branch of the company for which he worked, and nearing the end of it. Perhaps it had been this very knowledge of his imminent return to Canada which had precipitated matters between them. At twenty-three, Toni had never been short of men friends, but that was all they had meant to her to date. Randy was different. He demanded more from her than a simple semi-platonic relationship. When he told her he loved her his very ardour moved her not only to respond in kind but to believe it too.

His suggestion that she throw up her job and accompany him back to Canada had been phrased in such a manner as to offer what Toni had taken as a permanent arrangement. 'We can make a go of it,' he'd said persuasively. 'We've got what it takes. I can fix you a work permit.'

Until they started a family, Toni had thought, stifling any fleeting surprise. Most wives went out to a job these days—at least at first. Probably Randy believed she would prefer to retain that much independence, having been on her own since she was eighteen.

It was only on arrival in Vancouver that she finally realised marriage was not quite what Randy had had in mind. Even then she might eventually have gone along with things the way they were had his previous live-in companion not turned up, accompanied by the sixteen-month-old son for whom he was paying maintenance. He hadn't tried too hard to stop her walking out of his life, she had to admit.

The job in Vancouver had been by way of a stopgap until she could decide just what she was going to do with her life from here on in. Leaving it so abruptly after six short weeks had proved no real hardship because it had not been the kind of work for which she was really cut out. The decision to come east had been taken on impulse in the sudden surging desire to get away from the city which had brought her so much unhappiness. In hiring the car instead of taking train or plane, she had been submitting to a need for time in which to think. Last night she had spent in a motel near Kamloops, tonight she had hoped to make Golden. Motels were generally full by six in the evening, and already it was gone five. Perhaps this Clearwater place would offer some kind of accommodation, although as it wasn't even mentioned on the map it had to be tiny.

The sound of an engine brought her head up again. The truck came round the bend to pass her with a rush of displaced air, the driver's head swivelling to look at the ditched car. Toni turned at the sound of brakes being applied, and saw her antagonist of a moment ago standing out in the roadway waving the vehicle down. He was dressed, she noted irrelevantly, in slacks and a light shirt, the lowering sun outlining his tall, broad-shouldered frame against the snow-capped slopes of the mountains through which she had so recently travelled. He looked at home in the wilderness—big and grizzly as the bears against which she had been warned but not so far seen. Everything about this country was big, its very beauty was overwhelming. She felt a sudden pang of nostalgia for the flat Lincolnshire countryside of her birth.

The truck had stopped and the driver was getting down from the cab, as tall as the other man but with twice the girth. The confab was brief but obviously succinct, the newcomer nodding and swinging himself back up into the cab again as the younger man came back to where Toni still sat in the car. He was carrying a coil of rope in one hand, an end of which he proceeded to attach to her rear axle.

With the truck reversed as close to the ditched car as was possible, he made short work of coupling up the two vehicles, standing upright to view his handiwork with a satisfied nod of his head before coming on back to where Toni sat waiting.

'I'll take the wheel,' he said. 'The way you're angled

she could turn over without someone in there to steer her out.'

'In which case it's up to me to take the risk,' Toni pointed out, trying to sound calm and confident about it. 'I'll cope.'

The man's sigh was lacking in any kind of tolerance. 'I'm not standing around arguing the toss,' he said shortly. 'Either get out or I'll fetch you out.'

'You don't have any right——' she began, and broke off abruptly as he swung open her door in obvious intent. 'Just keep your hands to yourself!' she snapped, swinging her legs out from under the wheel. 'You go just a little too far!'

He ignored the last, dropping into the seat as she vacated it and closing the door against her. Fuming, she stood watching as he signalled to the truck driver, becoming aware for the first time of the various aches and pains from muscles strained in that final jolting ride into the ditch. There was a faint sense of nausea too—shock, in all probability. The last few minutes hadn't helped.

The convertible came out of the ditch with some reluctance, teetering on two nearside wheels for an instant before coming down on to level ground. The truck driver switched off his engine and got down to come back and lend a hand with the tow rope, running an appreciative eye over Toni as he did so.

'Have a blow-out?' he asked. 'Lucky you only finished up in the gully.'

Toni shook her head, conscious of the man nearby. 'Not a blow-out. I was just going too fast.'

'From England, aren't you?' he said, sounding uncommonly delighted. 'Say, what do you know! My folks are from your part of the world—Leeds. Do you know it?'

'Know of it. I've never been there myself.' Her smile was warm, the difference in this man's attitude almost compensating for the other. 'I'm from the south – at least, that's where I spent the last twelve years. Have you been over yet?'

'Never got round to it,' he admitted. 'Should have done it before the kids came along. Guess it'll have to wait till they're old enough to fend for themselves now.' He turned his attention to the other man, who had been looking around the car. 'Any damage?'

'Just a bent fender so far as I can see.' The grey eyes found Toni's, the expression in them heavy with irony. 'You've been lucky.'

'The devil looks after his own,' she retorted sweetly, and smiled again at the truck driver. 'Thanks a million for your help.'

'You're welcome,' he said. 'Mind how you go.'

'Advice you'd do well to heed,' commented the man left with her as the truck pulled away. 'Next time you might meet someone else with their mind on other things.'

'You've already made your point,' Toni came back on a hard note. 'You don't have to keep plugging it. If I thought all Canadians were like you I'd leave the country tomorrow—but fortunately I know they're not.' She walked over and got into the car, closing the door with control and reaching for the ignition. 'I'd thank you again for all your help,' she said, 'if I thought the gesture might be appreciated. Under the circumstances, I'll just say goodbye.'

He made no attempt to stop her as she disengaged the footbrake and put the car into motion. A couple of vehicles were coming up fast from the west. She let them both pass before pulling across to the right-hand lane and putting her foot down. Her last glimpse of the man was his back through her driving mirror as he walked to his own car parked facing west. And good riddance! she thought with feeling.

It was only when she saw the sign to Copper Lake some two miles or so farther on that she finally acknow-

ledged how badly her nerves had been affected by the
narrow scrape. The symbols said food and accommodation in addition to camping facilities, which meant at least
a bed for the night and a meal of sorts. She could fill up
in the morning and go right on through to Calgary, leaving herself with practically the whole weekend in which
to decide where she went from there. She certainly had to
make that decision soon. Her available cash would only
last her about another couple of weeks or so if she were to
leave herself enough for the plane fare home.

She had turned the car off the highway and on to the
narrow side road without having consciously made up her
mind. Driving north-east now she could see the mountain
ranges of Alberta lofting ahead, with one peak in particular standing clear, crested in its perpetual snows.
Between were the lower hills, pine-clad in green, the latter
broken only by small tracts of relatively open country like
oases in an undulating desert of trees.

It was in one of these that Copper Lake was situated.
Toni came on it suddenly round a bend in the road, looking down from above at the full length and breadth. The
lake was perhaps three-quarters of a mile long by a half a
mile wide at its farthest point, shaped like a pear with
trees coming right down to the water's edge along its right
bank. There were one or two scattered houses on the far
side, each with its own landing stage jutting into the
water. At this time of day, with the sun low down between
the peaks to the west, it was easy to see where the lake got
its name. The gleam on its surface was warmer than gold,
a deep glowing mirror stirred by not a single breath of
wind.

The lodge and trailer park were at this closest end.
From where she sat, Toni could make out three rows of
trailer hook-ups set at different levels into the hillside,
each site with its own picnic table and covered pergola.
The lodge complex itself was some few hundred yards

farther round the lake front, with neat little bungalows spreading into the trees beyond that. There were horses grazing in a fenced area down towards the lake, and small boats moored to a long stage. Of people she could see only one or two, but all the hook-ups were taken which seemed to indicate that the lodge too might be fully booked. She could only go on down and see.

The entrance to the site was just around the next corner, set ranch style beneath a timber canopy bearing the legend 'Copper Lake Lodge' burnt into it. A notice on the gatepost informed the reader that this gate would be closed between the hours of 11.00 p.m. and 7.00 a.m. To keep people in or out? Toni wondered whimsically.

There was a cattle grid across the opening, and beyond it a steepish lane leading down to a fork which went to the trailer park in one direction and the lodge proper in the other. From the number of cars already parked in the area provided for the purpose, the place was well on the way to a full capacity of guests. Toni could only hope that they might find room for a single. She badly needed a good night's sleep.

She found the lobby small but nicely furnished, with a polished maple reception desk towards the rear. The young woman on duty behind it shook her head ruefully in answer to Toni's request.

'I was just about to send someone along to put the "full" notice on the boards,' she said. 'We let the last room two minutes ago.'

'A cottage?' Toni ventured, hanging the costs, and received another sorrowful shake.

'They're long-term only—although I expect you could still have had one for the night if we'd one going spare.'

A bit of a pointless statement, Toni reflected, but refrained from saying so. The thought of making her way back to the main road and continuing her journey depressed her, but there was nothing else for it.

'Have you any idea how far it is to the next motel?' she asked wearily.

'Oh, that will be Golden. There's a trailer park just outside Clearview, but they don't have rooms.'

Golden was miles farther on. It would be almost seven by the time she got there, with no guarantee of finding a room going spare even then. But what other alternative did she have? Toni gave a rueful smile of her own as she began to turn away. 'Thanks anyway.'

'What's the trouble, Margot?' asked a new voice, and Toni turned back quickly to look at the man now framed in the opened doorway behind the girl.

'It's all right,' she said. 'No trouble. I wanted a room, that's all.'

'We're full,' supplied Margot unnecessarily.

'That's a pity.' The tone was sympathetic—more than that, it was concerned. 'Are you travelling alone?'

Toni nodded, as a faint element of hope sprang alive. If this was the manager, he might be able to swing something. Anything rather than drive any farther tonight. True, he didn't look like a manager. No older than herself, and dressed in jeans and a check shirt, he looked more like one of the campers than a man responsible for the running of the place.

'I'd take anything,' she said. 'I'd sleep on a pool table if the chance were offered!'

A grin lit the thin tanned features. 'The serious players might object. Anyway, we might be able to do a bit better than that.' His glance returned to the receptionist. 'What about number thirteen?'

She looked doubtful. 'We don't normally let that.'

'I'm not superstitious,' put in Toni, and drew another smile from her benefactor.

'Not so much the problem. The cottage is one left from the previous owner's days. It's just one room with a shower which doesn't work—though it does have hot and cold water on tap. No cooking facilities either, which seems to be its main drawback. We keep it purely for emergencies.'

'This is one,' Toni assured him. 'I'm tired and hungry and I don't mind what it's like providing there's a bed. You do have a dining room here, don't you?'

'Sure thing.' He had come forward to the desk, his glance lingering on the honey-coloured sweep of her hair for a fleeting moment of unmasked admiration. 'It's going to take a little time to get the place ready for occupation. If you want to wash up before you eat you can use one of the lodge bathrooms. Dinner's from six to seven-thirty.'

'Oh, that's wonderful! Thank you.' Her gratitude was probably out of all proportion considering she would be paying for the accommodation, but Toni ignored the fact. She *was* grateful. If it wasn't for this man's timely intervention she would still be minus a place to stay. 'I'll just go out and get my handgrip, then I'll be ready to take you up on that offer to use a bathroom.'

'You'd better register first,' said the receptionist, already filling in the appropriate line in the book. 'Number thirteen is fifteen dollars a night.'

'Make it ten,' ordered the man at her side. 'It isn't worth more.' He watched Toni sign her name, added lightly, 'Miss or Mrs Bradbury?'

'Miss,' she said, too well aware that his interest was not purely of a business nature. She laid down the pen and looked up to meet the hazel eyes for a brief moment, struck by something vaguely familiar about the thin, attractively boyish face. 'Are you the manager here?'

'Owner-manager,' he corrected. 'Part owner, anyway. It's a family concern.' He held out a hand. 'Sean Stewart.'

Toni shook hands, amused by the unexpected formality. Perhaps he considered it was only what an English girl would expect from a man.

'I'll get my things,' she repeated.

There was no sign of rain in the cloudless blue of the evening sky, but she put the top up on the car just in case. There were one or two boats out on the lake—fishermen by the look of them. No doubt that was the main source of entertainment. Caught against the backdrop of mountains, the whole scene offered peace and tranquillity of a kind which was balm to her injured spirit. It would have been nice, she thought, to have stayed here for a while if she'd the time to spare.

So why didn't she make the time? came the immediate question. If she needed a couple of days in which to think things out surely this place was better than Calgary? The car wasn't due to be turned in until Tuesday as she had wanted time to drive around the city and get her bearings before resorting to public transport. If she left here early Monday morning she could be in Calgary by evening, and perhaps with a much clearer mind. The idea was worth considering.

She was still considering it when she sat down to dinner in the bright and comfortable dining room, but by the end of the main course of baked trout had definitely made up her mind. The food was excellent, and not at all expensively priced. Three nights here would certainly be a great deal less costly than the same in Calgary.

Sean Stewart came over to her table while she was still drinking coffee, ostensibly to enquire how she had enjoyed her meal. He had changed into light linen slacks and long-sleeved shirt in a pale fawn which enhanced both the tan of his features and the darkness of his hair. A very good-looking young man, Toni reflected, and fairly well aware of it, yet endearingly lacking in the peacock-type vanity which often accompanied such awareness.

'I'll take you across and show you where you'll be spending the night whenever you're ready,' he offered. 'I only wish we had better accommodation to offer you.'

'Beggars can't be choosers,' she reminded him. 'Stop worrying about it. I'm sure everything will be fine.' She paused there for a moment, glancing out through the wide windows to the lake and the grazing horses. 'As a matter of fact, I'm thinking of staying the weekend,' she added. 'Will there be any spare rooms here in the lodge, do you think?'

'Oh, yes, sure.' He sounded pleased—almost eager. 'I can check you in first thing in the morning as soon as the first lot leaves. Number three already asked for a wake-up call at six-thirty.'

'I shan't be in that much of a hurry,' Toni assured him. 'In fact, I might even prefer to stay right where I am.'

'More convenient over here,' he rejoined. 'Especially if you plan to take all your meals in the dining room. We do a full breakfast menu, English style and Continental.'

'Toast and coffee will be enough for me.' She studied him for a moment, attempting to pin down the elusive familiarity, without success. 'Won't you sit down while you're waiting?' she asked, shelving the question as of little import. 'I'm enjoying this too much to hurry over it.'

'Please don't,' he hastened to assure her, taking her at her word. 'In fact, I'll join you.' He signalled the waitress and ordered fresh coffee for them both, then sat back in his seat to view her with obvious pleasure. 'You know, it isn't all that often we have any British staying. Are you just visiting Canada or do you plan on staying some time?'

'I'm not sure,' she admitted. 'I came over with that intention, but——' She broke off abruptly, conscious of having already said more than she had intended. 'I thought of getting a job in Calgary for a few months,' she went on after a moment. 'Have you any idea what secretarial opportunities might be like?'

'Extremely good, especially for somebody with training.

You'll be snapped up,' Sean declared with a certainty which made her smile.

'How can you be sure I'm so well qualified?' she asked, tongue in cheek.

'The look of you. The way you talk. Mind you,' he added in perfect seriousness, 'I had you down for a photographic model up until now. You've got the bone structure for it.'

Her brows lifted a fraction. 'You know something about photography?'

'I've dabbled a bit. Margot—the girl on reception—sits for me sometimes. Only a hobby, of course—although I do my own developing and enlarging. Gives me some interest outside of all this,' with a gesture which encompassed the whole of the site visible from where they sat. 'You've no idea how limiting this job can be.'

'You said it was a family concern,' Toni murmured. 'Do they leave you to manage the place on your own?'

'Apart from frequent visits by big brother.' The statement held a certain rancour. 'Rafe has a lot more on his plate than I have. I guess I should be thankful for small mercies.' Seeing the genuine interest in the green eyes opposite he became suddenly confiding. 'We're a pretty well diversified company. Too many fingers in too many pies, some might say. Rafe takes care of everything apart from this side. It's supposed to be totally my concern. Only thing is, I don't seem to have what it takes to devote my life to fishing and winter sports, and that's about what it amounts to. Come November I'll be back up at Valemont where our Company owns a ski lodge looking forward to another season of après-ski evenings and fun-filled days. We've extended too this year. There isn't going to be time to breathe, let alone anything else.'

Toni studied him thoughtfully, aware that the lightness was merely donned for the occasion. 'If you feel so out of place doing what you are doing why don't you let your brother run the Lodges and take over some other facet of the company?' she asked, and saw his shoulders lift wryly.

'Wouldn't work. I've tried. Motel management is about the closest I've come to making a good job, and even that leaves a lot to be desired.'

'According to whom?'

'Rafe. My mother. Me too, if it comes to that.'

'Then do something else outside the company.'

'Such as?'

'Oh, lord, I don't know. I've no idea of your capabilities.' Toni was beginning to be sorry she had allowed herself to become involved. 'Photography, perhaps, if that's what you're interested in.'

'Hardly a paying concern unless it's the big commercial stuff, and I can't afford to take the chance on getting that far.' He caught her eye and shrugged again. 'My share dividends are all tied up until I'm twenty-five, and until then I'm purely on salary like any other employee. Compliments of my father. He did the same for Rafe, to be fair, only he reached his majority nine years ago.'

She was getting in too deep too fast, Toni told herself, yet having come this far she hardly felt able to back out now. Sean was obviously lost for a willing ear. Even talking out his problems might help to ease them.

'I take it your brother isn't here at present,' she said.

'He left for Vancouver a couple of hours ago. Going to pick up a new plane. The old one got bent.'

A private plane? Toni mentally shrugged. Why not? From what she had already heard, the Stewart Company was more than a going concern. Something was growing at the back of her mind, reaching a near certainty as she looked once more at the face across the table from her.

'Was he by any chance driving a white Buick?' she heard herself asking, and knew the answer before it came.

'That's right. Hey, how did you know that?'

Her smile was faint. 'You could say we almost bumped

into one another a couple of miles back along the Highway. I thought you looked somehow familiar when I first arrived—family resemblance.'

'You certainly managed to notice a lot from a passing car,' Sean commented curiously, and she laughed without humour.

'I had a close-up in more ways than one. I ran off the road and he came back to rescue me. Considering it was my fault we nearly collided, I suppose I can't blame him too much for feeling the way he obviously did.'

'Meaning he read you the riot act?' Sean's smile was ruefully reminiscent. 'He sure can go to town on that. Bet you didn't just sit there and take it, though.'

'I was too shocked to say much,' Toni admitted. 'By the near miss, I mean. That's the main reason I came in here for a room. I was feeling a bit too shaken up to drive through to Golden tonight.'

'And that brother of mine wouldn't have helped any.' He sounded suddenly angry. 'Sometimes he's just a mite too fast on the jump!'

'It doesn't matter now,' Toni hastened to reassure him. 'I'm over it. I don't suppose he'll be coming back this weekend?'

'Hardly. Should be six weeks or so before he makes another visit. He seemed to think things were going reasonably well.'

'Only reasonably?'

'That's Rafe. Super-efficient himself, and expects everyone else to follow suit.'

Toni could imagine. It suited her impression of the man she had met so briefly. She drained her coffee cup and pushed back her chair. 'I'll need my case from the car.'

The cottage she had been allocated was tucked away in the trees at the far end of the group, at some considerable distance from the Lodge. By British standards, the single room was not only adequate in size but quite well equipped with table and chairs in addition to the two divan beds, one of which was still made up as a seating unit. There was a loop-piled carpet covering the floor and fresh blue and white cotton curtains at the two windows. A small closet-like area partitioned off at the back held the shower and toilet.

'I don't see what you were worried about,' Toni admitted frankly to Sean when he once more apologised for his inability to provide anything better. 'It's clean, it's perfectly comfortable and at ten dollars a night it's a snap. With a small extension on the back to hold a kitchen and a proper bathroom, there's no reason why it shouldn't be as going a concern as the others obviously are. I'm surprised your brother hasn't thought of it.'

'He has.' Sean looked a little sheepish. 'One of the things I was supposed to organise before the season got under way. But in the rush to get the new units up and functioning in time, I somehow forgot to tell the builders to make over this place at the same time. Have to wait now.'

'If you only built the cottages this year you've done well to get full capacity bookings this early in June,' she commented. 'Good P.R., or did you just rely on luck?'

Sean smiled. 'The Stewarts never rely on luck. How about coming across for a drink before you turn in?'

'You have a bar?' Toni queried, surprised.

'Not a public one—we don't have a liquor licence. I meant to my place. I've a couple of rooms at the back for my own use. I don't have too much of a choice to offer, but I can probably find something you'll like.'

'I don't think so, thanks. Not tonight.' Toni kept her tone light. 'I'm too tired to even think straight, much less walk up to the Lodge again.' She paused before adding casually, 'Are the horses just for decoration, or can I get a ride?'

'Any time you like.' Sean wasn't bothering to hide his

disappointment. 'There's a party of three going out at nine-thirty in the morning. Shall I tell Bill to count you in?'

She hesitated. 'I'd prefer to go out alone.'

'Can't be done—lodge rules. Too many places a horse can break a leg round here, to say nothing of its rider's neck.'

'I can ride,' she protested mildly.

'Western style?'

'That too. My last employer kept a small stable for family use. I had free access.'

Sean looked doubtful. 'I still don't think Bill would go for it. At least, not before he's seen how you handle a horse. His family's back in Kamloops. I guess the horses are a kind of substitute. He's an ex-rodeo rider, and a real character. You'd get along fine.'

Toni shrugged and gave in, unwilling to make an issue of something so relatively unimportant. Anyway, she could see some sense in what Sean had said. She didn't know the country. 'All right, tell him I'll be there. What time is breakfast, by the way?'

'From seven-thirty to nine. There'll be a room with a shower vacant after eight if you want to come over and use it. We can always bring your bags over later.'

'Thanks, but I'll bathe in the lake for one morning,' she said. 'It looks good and clean.'

'Ninety-six point six pollution free at the last test,' he agreed with an element of pride. He waited a brief moment before taking the hint implicit in her concealed yawn, moving with reluctance to the door. 'I'll leave you to it, then. Hope you manage a good night's sleep.'

Alone at last, Toni breathed a small sigh of relief and began to unpack what few things she would need for the coming weekend. She had been telling the truth when she said she was tired, but she would have refused Sean's invitation anyway. He was nice, and in many ways she felt sorry for him, only that didn't mean that she wanted to become any more involved in his problems than she already was. She was here for a quiet weekend, and that was all.

That brother of his really took the prize for sheer, cold-blooded indifference, though. Why press someone into a job for which they were temperamentally unsuited when it was more than obvious that the Company could well afford to put in a manager to run the Lodges? Sean deserved a better deal than the one he had been landed with.

She was doing it again, she realised with a wry shake of her head. The Stewart Company policies were none of her concern. If Sean wanted out it was up to him to stand up for his rights. Except that a man like Rafe Stewart would not be easy to stand against, she had to acknowledge. She could only be thankful that she would not be meeting him again.

CHAPTER TWO

THE morning was bright and cloudless, the heat already beginning to dance off the water when Toni went down to bathe at seven-thirty. She found the lake surprisingly warm considering its height above sea level.

Several other people had had the same idea. Toni got into conversation with a young German couple from one of the motor-homes, and agreed with them that Canada was one beautiful country.

'The scenery is almost too much at times,' declared the man, whose name was Claus. 'It numbs the senses. We have taken so many photographs of mountains we shall have to buy more film here before we leave.'

Not owning a camera, Toni had taken none, but she knew just what he meant. One wanted to preserve every moment, every vivid impression. The trouble was the average amateur snapshot scarcely did justice to reality. Better to buy the professionally finished postcards and send them home franked from each stop if a true representation were required.

At eight-thirty she went across for breakfast, meeting a despondent-looking Sean in the lobby on the way out again.

'Afraid your ride's off,' he announced glumly. 'Bill was called away early this morning—family problems. Leaves us high and dry till he can get back. There's nobody else available to take the rides out.'

'I'd still like to go,' she said. 'I'll be perfectly safe if I watch my trail. I daresay the horses know the routes as well as anybody, if it comes to that.' The doubt still in his expression brought a measure of impatience. 'Look, come with me if you're so worried about your animals.'

'I was thinking more about you,' he came back on a hurt note which made her feel more than a little ashamed of her sharpness. The movement of his shoulders was rueful. 'Nothing I'd like better than to oblige, but horses just aren't my thing, I'm afraid. I'm strictly a car man.' He paused again, then gave in. 'They're still up in the top corral. If you go and choose which one you want to ride I'll have it brought down and saddled for you.'

'I can do that,' she offered. 'I'd like to.'

'Well, I'll come up with you anyway,' he said, obviously still not totally convinced that he was doing the right thing. 'Could be you'll need help rounding them up. Bill always says they're like anybody else—reluctant to start work of a morning. Are you ready now?'

Toni was wearing the jeans, shirt and sneakers which was standard riding uniform in this part of the world. She nodded. 'Quite ready.'

The top corral was up by the main gate. Not a particularly safe place to keep valuable animals overnight, she would have thought, but perhaps horse thieves weren't a problem. There were six in all, ranging from a rangy chestnut through to a little Apaloosa mare Sean told her could go like the wind. One of the geldings in particular caught her eye. He was a big grey named appropriately Silver, in beautiful condition and with the powerful hindquarters of a latent jumper.

'I'll take him,' said Toni.

Sean sighed. 'Sorry, there I have to draw the line. He's Bill's ride—a one-man horse. Any of the others, but not Silver.'

There was a challenge in that statement, but Toni refrained from acting on it. Sean had made one concession already; it would hardly be fair to press him to make another.

She chose the bigger of the two palominos in the end, clicking her fingers and saying his name reassuringly as she moved to cut him off from the other animals in the corral. Duke stood still on her approach, ears flicking to the sound of her voice. Still without moving, he allowed her to slide the rope halter over his head.

Sean was admiring when she brought the animal out of the corral. 'You really do have a way with horses, don't you?' he said. 'Even Bill usually takes longer than that to get a rope on.'

'It's all in the tone,' she smiled back. 'Hit the right note and the rest is easy.'

The tack was stored in a shed down by the enclosure where the animals had been grazing the previous evening. Even carrying one of the Western saddles was quite a feat, as they weighed a great deal more than their English counterparts with all the extra leather. Sitting in one was like sitting in a cradle, in Toni's estimation, although she had to admit they were comfortable.

The three children who were booked for the nine-thirty ride turned up as Sean was giving her a leg up into the saddle. They looked so despondent on being given the news that Toni was moved to an impulsive offer.

'Once I've got my bearings I could take them out for an hour,' she said to Sean, and countered his unspoken objection by adding swiftly, 'There were three children in the family I worked for down in Vancouver, and all younger than these. I'm capable—really.'

'I believe it.' He was smiling now, and looking more than a little relieved. 'Hardly fair to break in on your weekend, though.'

'I don't mind,' she assured him. 'I enjoy riding any time.' She looked back to the three waiting figures. 'Come on down right after lunch and you'll get your ride.'

'Thanks,' Sean said gratefully, walking a short distance alongside as she moved towards the gate at the far end of the pasture. 'I'll call round and see if I can find some temporary help while you're out. Mind how you go.'

She laughed and lifted a hand in salute before urging the gelding on with a touch of her heels against the silken sides. Western trained horses did not respond to knee pressure, nor did they like any pull on the mouth unless in a request to stop. One rode with two loose reins gathered in the one hand and guided the animal by a simple left or right movement which touched the leather lightly along the appropriate side of the neck. It had taken her some time to adjust her ideas, and even now she would have preferred a two-handed control, if only in that it gave her more communication with the animal under her. On a morning like this, however, it was enough just to be mounted again. She felt totally content.

As she had predicted, Duke seemed to know which way to head, angling up the hillside and along a well worn trail through the trees to emerge eventually on a plateau flat enough and open enough to afford space for a gallop. Reining in at the far end where the trail entered the tree line again, Toni sat for a moment or two just looking at the view. The lake was below and behind her now, while in front and to either side stretched a landscape which caught at her throat. A few miles away another lake glinted under the sun against the backdrop of white-capped mountains. Up there the snows were eternal, the rock below unchanged and unchanging through thousands of years. The emotion swelling in her was so intense that for a fleeting moment it was almost tangible. Happiness: pure unadulterated happiness.

It didn't last, of course. Not at the same peak. There were too many things waiting to drag her down again. Only not as far, because she wouldn't let herself dwell on them. She was making a new start from this moment on.

She took the three children out that afternoon as promised, and thoroughly enjoyed every minute of the hour. When asked by others on their return if she would be taking out any further rides that day, she could only shake her head with regret and refer them to the manager, who might by this time have come up with some solution.

Sean, however, had not. His stint on the telephone had been in vain.

'Guess we're just going to have to put them out to pasture till Bill gets back,' he said wryly, when Toni came across him in the store where she had gone to buy an ice. 'Won't make all that much difference to profits, I suppose. It's the guests who are going to miss the facility—especially as it's underlined in the brochures as an added incentive to stay at Copper Lake.'

'Yes,' Toni agreed, 'it's a shame. Still, it might not be for too long.'

'It depends on what's gone wrong.' There was a pause while he studied her, a new expression coming into his eyes. When he spoke again it was hesitantly, as if he already heard her refusal in his mind. 'I don't suppose you'd consider taking the job on, would you? After all, you don't have one to go to, and Calgary will still be there a couple of weeks from now.'

Toni stood with the ice-cream cone suspended halfway to her lips while she considered the idea. She had to admit that it had its attractions. Two or three weeks in this place doing work she loved could be just what the doctor ordered.

The elation lasted bare seconds before memory returned. 'I can't,' she said with regret. 'I have to return my car on Tuesday.'

'I'll cover the hire charges while you're here in addition to salary.' His tone was eager. 'You'd be living rent free, so you'd come out well on top.' He seized on her hesitancy, a plea in his eyes. 'You've no idea how you'd be helping. If word gets around that promised facilities might not be forthcoming we stand to lose bookings. Folks want certainty—especially the long-term guests. We would lose a whole lot of goodwill.'

The hesitation was still there, but for a different reason this time. 'What about your brother?' asked Toni.

'What about him? He'd be only too glad I'd found somebody to take over.'

'That wasn't what I meant.' She paused, seeing the sardonic twist of firm lips in her mind's eye and feeling the same angry response run through her. 'I wouldn't want to run foul of him again,' she said. 'Once was more than enough.'

'There's no chance of that,' Sean returned, accepting her comment in the manner of one who perfectly understood that kind of reticence. 'He won't be here again for at least six weeks. So far as he'll be concerned, you'll just be a name on the staff list when he does see it. By that time you'll be in Calgary.'

She made the decision swiftly, aware that if she stopped to think too hard and too long about it she might find other difficulties in the way. 'All right, I'll do it. Starting right now, if you like. There's another party wanting to go.'

'That's great!' He was all boyish enthusiasm. 'That's just great! We can discuss salary when you get back. I promise you won't be disappointed.'

'I'd better not be.' She was laughing, pleased herself at the way things had turned out. 'Riding mistress at Copper Lake. It sounds rather grand, doesn't it!'

The pleasure in no way decreased over the following days, busy as Toni was kept. Riding was a popular pastime for young and not so young alike, and there were times when she felt bound to limit the number of rides in order to give the animals adequate rest.

Offered the opportunity to move into the Lodge house itself, she had requested instead to stay where she was in the end cottage, preferring the relative privacy of the situation. With the lake practically on the doorstep, the lack of a proper bathroom was no real drawback, and she was spared the sounds from the jukebox disco which took place twice a week until eleven in the recreation room.

The disco was not the only source of evening entertainment. On the Saturday there had been a barbecue which everyone attended, either cooking their own food on the charcoal grills provided, or participating in the group event arranged by the Lodge staff. A regular feature of the summer season, Toni learned, and one which was always well appreciated. She looked forward to the next with anticipation.

Sean had become a good friend, and she was careful to keep the relationship on that basis. Being unattracted towards him in any physical sense, she found his companionship no threat to her equanimity, and was quite happy to spend most evenings chatting amicably about this and that, either on their own or on occasion with others who might wander into their sphere. To Sean's state of mind she gave little thought because he never made an issue of it himself. He seemed perfectly content with things the way they were.

When he asked her if she would sit for a couple of photographs she was happy enough to oblige and was pleasantly impressed by the finished result. Sean had a flair for lighting his subjects, subtly emphasising the better features and playing down the rest. She had no bad side at all, he told her—a perfect oval of a face with just enough prominence of the cheekbones to lend interesting hollows below. If she had a fault of any kind it might be that aesthetically her eyes were just a fraction too long, and very slightly slanted, but that, he assured her, added to rather than detracted from the overall impression.

'Perhaps there's some Chinese in my ancestry,' riposted Toni lightly. 'My mother's mother was Italian, so I'm already something of a mixture.'

Sean's glance was curious. 'You've never mentioned your family before. I thought you mightn't have parents alive.'

Her shrug held a nonchalance assumed for the occasion. 'They're divorced, and my mother is dead now. I very rarely see my father.'

'You poor kid!' It could have sounded ridiculous considering the bare four months difference in their ages, instead the softly spoken comment melted a small portion of that hard little core deep down inside her. For the first time in years she found herself actually wanting to talk about it.

'It happened a long time ago,' she said. 'I lived with Dad till I was seventeen, then he met Jennifer and—well, we just didn't get along too well, that's all. Jealousy on my part, perhaps. Anyway, I found myself a job in London and shared a flat with two other girls until I was making enough to get a place of my own.'

'And he didn't try to stop you going?'

'Yes, he tried. But he was between two fires. If I'd stayed I don't think Jennifer would have married him.'

'Jealously on her part, maybe?'

'In a way I suppose it was. It was her first marriage, and she's quite a bit younger than Dad. They've two children of their own now.'

'And even less room for a grown-up sister.' His hands were light as he drew her towards him to rest his cheek against her hair. 'Poor abandoned little Toni!'

She should move away, Toni knew, yet the sheer comfort of his arms about her was more than she could resist. When he moved his head to kiss her she responded without thinking about it, only breaking away when the pressure advanced beyond the realms of sympathy.

'I'm sorry,' she said wryly. 'I didn't mean that to happen.'

'I did.' Sean was smiling. 'That's the first time you've

really opened up, Toni. I hope it's not the last.'

Whatever she might have said in reply to that was lost as the noise from outside impinged upon her consciousness. Sean seemed to hear it at the same moment, and his expression went an abrupt and singular change.

'That's a plane,' he said. 'And it's coming in to land.'

Rafe Stewart. Toni's heart did a sudden double beat, then steadied again as she brought herself sharply under control. So what if it was? She was doing a bona fide job here, and doing it well. Whatever his opinion of her as a driver, he could scarcely quarrel with her proven ability over the last week.

Sean had gone to the window of the sitting room which served double duty as studio, craning his neck to watch the bright blue and white machine descend towards the landing strip laid out beyond the belt of trees.

'It's Rafe,' he stated flatly. 'One of his surprise visits planned to catch me slacking on the job!'

'Or perhaps just to show you his new machine,' suggested Toni, not really believing it herself. 'After all, he'd surely not fly all this way up from Vancouver just to catch you out?'

'Not just,' Sean agreed. 'He'll be on his way back to Calgary. No need to drop in at all, considering he was here just a week back, but that's Rafe. Never misses an opportunity.'

In which case Sean should have been expecting this, Toni thought, but refrained from voicing any comment.

'I'll see you later,' she said. 'I've a ride to take out at four.'

With any luck, Rafe Stewart would be gone by the time she got back at five. No doubt he had business to catch up on. It was the first time she had realised that the family was actually based in Calgary—at least that was the impression she had received from what Sean had said just now. And waiting at home was the mother—the matriarch. The true ruler of the Stewart clan, perhaps? From what she could recall of the elder son, Toni doubted it.

She was late returning from the ride owing to the Apaloosa throwing a shoe. Tucked away behind the trees, the landing strip had not been visible even from the top of the hill. Toni could only hope that the visitor had departed. A confrontation with the man she remembered so well was the last thing she felt like tonight.

Her hopes, however, were soon to be dashed. The two brothers came strolling across to the saddling rail as Toni brought her charges safely in through the gate at the rear of the pasture, the taller of the two moving to inspect the big grey and the chestnut still tied up there. His expression on looking up to her approach was more than enough to tell her that whatever details Sean had seen fit to impart regarding their new riding instructor, that previous meeting had not been among them. She got in first before he could speak, driven by a need to impress upon him her total lack of concern over the unfortunate event.

'Good afternoon, Mr Stewart,' she said formally. 'I hope we haven't been keeping you waiting. Bonny has a loose shoe.'

He said nothing, waiting until the riders had dispersed and all the horses were tied before finally giving voice to the words she could almost hear quivering in the air.

'I'm not sure what your game is,' he said on a clipped note, 'but I'm going to find out. Why here, of all places?'

'Why anywhere?' she asked, fighting the desire to demand what he thought her game *might* be. 'I was tired and shaken up, and this place just happened to be handy.'

'That was a week ago.'

'So why am I still here?' She was leaning against the rail with a hand on Duke's soft nose, stroking him almost unconsciously. 'I'd have thought that was obvious. Sean needed a temporary relief and I didn't have anything special to do for a week or two, so here I am.'

'So I see.' His tone was not encouraging. 'With what qualifications?'

'Nothing on paper,' she admitted. 'I wasn't aware it was necessary to the job.'

'Meaning anybody can control a team of animals ridden mainly by amateurs?'

'No, that's not what I meant.' Her own control was fast slipping. 'But an experienced enough rider can do it without a certificate of merit. My last employers trusted me to take their three young children out without supervision.'

'On horseback?'

'Yes, on horseback.' She was sharp, sensing some underlying motive in the question. 'The family owned a livery stable.'

'Why did you leave?' This time the question was soft.

Toni stiffened, eyes suddenly veiled. 'Personal reasons,' she said shortly.

Sean chose that moment to step in, face stiff. 'Isn't that enough of the inquisition, Rafe?' he demanded. 'Toni helped me out in a bad situation. And she handles horses as if she was born to it.'

Grey eyes did not move from green. 'All right,' he said, 'so give me a demonstration. We'll go out now, just the two of us. These two are fresh,' indicating the grey and the chestnut. 'You can unsaddle the others and leave them free to graze.' He paused. 'Mind telling me why these two were left tied in the first place?'

'Because Silver is more than capable of jumping the fence to follow,' Toni responded stiffly, 'and Caspar would have followed him. I don't think riderless animals are very helpful on a ride.'

The sarcasm was ignored. 'He's Bill's lead horse. He's used to going out with every ride. Why don't you use him?'

It would have been simple enough to tell the truth, that she was still feeling her way with the big animal, and only used him where necessity dictated on the actual rides. To anyone else, that was. This man was different. Explanations would be regarded as excuses. Toni lifted her shoulders.

'I prefer a change.'

'I'm sure you do.' His tone was smooth—too smooth. 'Right, let's get the others unsaddled before we go.'

Toni caught Sean's eye as his brother turned away, and warmed as always to the concern in them. The brief shake of her head was to dissuade him from any further intervention on her behalf. She would handle this herself. Whatever happened, Rafe Stewart was not going to undermine her confidence.

Dressed today in well-cut jeans and a blue cotton shirt, he looked subtly different from the man she had met a week ago. Apart from his expression, that was. Did the man ever relax and smile with genuine warmth instead of that mocking flicker? Perhaps he just didn't like women, she reflected dryly as she slid off Duke's saddle and hung it over the rail to air off. Some men didn't basically, even though quite prepared to take advantage of their physical uses. Let down once by the opposite sex, a few weak characters remained scarred for life by the experience. Except that she somehow couldn't imagine this man having any weaknesses. He suggested strength through and through.

With the other animals turned loose to graze, it took Toni bare moments to saddle up the two left. Rafe made no attempt to help her, watching her movements with that same cynical look about his mouth.

'No,' he said when she made a move towards the chestnut. 'You ride Silver.'

Toni obeyed without change of expression, vaulting lightly into the saddle before either man could offer her a leg up. From her vantage point she looked down at the

two, closing one eye in a swift wink for Sean's benefit
when the other man moved to mount the chestnut. Don't
worry, she was saying in effect, I don't mind humouring
him.

'Back in half an hour or so,' said Rafe in the saddle. 'It
shouldn't take longer than that.'

There was something vaguely disturbing in the way he
brought out those last few words—something Toni
couldn't quite put her finger on. She felt suddenly that
there was more to this outing of theirs than met the eye.

She rode in front of him along the lane and up the
bank to the first of the three gates which had to be opened
en route, managing to back Silver up with only little
difficulty as she held on to the wood. Once through it had
to be closed again under Rafe's gaze. It was in some relief
that she dropped the wire closure back over the post and
turned her horse's head to the uphill trail.

There was no comment from behind during the first
half mile. Only when they entered the belt of trees towards
the top of the hill did he suggest with irony that she might
try to avoid letting the overreaching branches spring back
too quickly from her grasp.

It had been a genuine accident in that the said bunch
of foliage had slipped through her fingers, but there was
little point in saying so. Toni gritted her teeth and carried
on, aware in every fibre of the tall lean figure at her back.
At least Silver was behaving himself up to now, moving
ahead decorously to her guidance. Perhaps after all she
had done the wrong thing in not riding him from the first.
All they had needed was a certain rapport, and that they
appeared to have achieved.

It was tempting providence, of course, in the way over-
confidence always does. Sensing a certain relaxation in
her watchfulness, the grey chose that moment to revert to
type, breaking into a canter without any urging and
taking the next small fallen log across the trail in an almost

deliberately mistimed jump which very nearly unseated her. It took her some moments to pull him up because she couldn't get a proper hold on his mouth using the one hand only. Finally she took a rein in each and did it the British way, hauling back strongly and steadily until the animal got it into his head that he was not going to get his way.

'You goof!' she exclaimed in angry exasperation when they came to a halt. 'Of all the times in the world to start playing up you had to choose this one! You must be in cahoots, you two. You both want me to fall on my face!'

The grey, quite naturally, said nothing, standing quietly now, ears flicking to the sound of her voice. When he swung the great head round to look at her it was with such a quizzical gleam in his eye that Toni had to laugh. 'Devil!' she said, leaning forward to slide a hand over the smooth neck. 'I'll master you yet!'

'I doubt it,' commented Rafe, arriving in time to hear the last words. 'I'd say he just proved that much.'

'I pulled him up,' she pointed out, hanging on to her temper.

'Having let him go in the first place.' The dark head was cocked, his mouth slanted to match. 'How about if you'd had a string of beginners behind you, then? The others will follow the leader's pace automatically, you know that. It could have meant a fall.'

'But it didn't because they weren't,' she retorted ungrammatically. 'You're just looking for excuses, Mr Stewart!'

He had ridden up close, his knee on a level with hers as he brought his mount head to tail with Silver. The grey eyes held a curious expression. 'Excuses for what?'

'To get rid of me.' She was too angry and upset to pay much heed to what she was saying. 'The very fact that Sean offered me the job without waiting to consult you first was enough, wasn't it? He's supposed to be in complete charge of this part of the business, yet you won't even leave him free to make his own decisions!'

His eyes had narrowed, the expression in them hardening dangerously. 'You and he seem to have done quite a lot of getting together this past week,' he said. 'One way and another.'

Toni flushed. 'What's that supposed to mean?'

'You tell me. I've seen the photographs he did of you, and Margot on reception tells me you've spent every evening together. How about the nights?'

Toni drew in a sharp breath, the flush deepening. When she did speak it was in a tone as cold as she could make it. 'If you had any right to ask I wouldn't be obliged to answer. Your brother is a grown man, not a child to be taken care of!'

'My brother is twenty-three,' he answered with deliberation, 'and as naïve as they come when a pretty face is involved. Not his fault. He never learned to look any farther.'

'While you did, of course.' Her own lip had curled. 'All the same under the skin, are we, Mr. Stewart?'

He had hold of her before she guessed his intention, his hand hard behind her head as he drew her bodily towards him almost out of the saddle. His mouth was hard too, but in a quite different way. She couldn't fight it, only suffer it, her whole body tensed to his touch.

When he let her go she put up her hand and quite deliberately wiped the back of it across her lips, not bothering to conceal her revulsion.

'That's probably all you know,' she said with contempt.

'It's all you merit,' he came back on a biting note. 'Craig Shannon's a grown man too. Is that the only criterion you need?'

The flush faded abruptly, leaving her pale for a moment by comparison. She gazed at him in silence, unable to find any words which might sort out the confusion in her mind. When she did manage to speak it was not at all what she had really meant to say.

'What do you know about Craig Shannon?'

'He's a friend. He and his wife.' He paused to let the words sink in, registering her reactions with a twist of his lips. 'I was there a couple of days ago. Diane told me about their children's errant nanny. She even showed me a photograph of her taken with the kids. So cut up about it, she was. She'd liked the girl so much. Who would have thought a girl like that would stab her in the back by trying to entice her own husband?' The laugh was brief and harsh. 'Who but Diane would have thought she wouldn't!'

The utter coincidence of it all took Toni's breath. Things like this just didn't happen in real life! But they did. Of course they did. Wasn't it only a month ago at the top of Grouse Mountain when she had turned to the sound of a familiar voice to find herself looking into the equally amazed face of a one-time next-door neighbour of her parents? For two people to travel thousands of miles at different times and yet meet up in the same spot at a given moment in time was unbelievable in itself. Why should this be so much more? The Shannons and the Stewarts moved in the same spheres. It had to be conceivable that they might have met.

'No ready answer?' The mockery cut through her thoughts like a red hot iron. 'Shame. I'd an idea you knew them all!'

'It wasn't——' she began, then broke off abruptly. Why should she try to defend herself against this man's obvious pre-judgment? Yet could she really blame him for thinking the way he did? He had heard only one side of the story—the side Craig must have seen fit to pass on to his wife in explanation of her sudden decision to leave. Entice him indeed! The shoe had been on the other foot.

'Wasn't what?' Rafe prompted. 'Intentional? You were carried away by sudden overwhelming emotion, was that it?'

Toni discarded any idea she might have had of trying to explain. He wasn't going to believe her, no matter how she put it across. She shook her head wearily. 'It hardly matters now. I left the place before any damage was done.'

'The same way you're leaving this one.' His tone was hard. 'I brought you up here to say what had to be said out of Sean's hearing. When we get back I'll expect you to be packed and off the premises before nightfall.'

She looked at him for a long moment, searching without much hope for any sign of a kink in the armour. 'What do I tell Sean?' she asked at last.

'You don't have to tell him anything. Let him think I'm firing you because you're just not good enough. It's close enough to the truth.'

She made no answer to that; there seemed no point. Head up, she indicated the way they had come. 'Perhaps you'd like to lead the way down again. I might just feel tempted to let a few more branches back in your face!'

'Try it,' he invited pleasantly, 'and you'll get more than you bargained for. Might do you good at that. Lead on, honey, I'll be right behind you.'

They reached base in a silence broken only by the normal sounds of the landscape going on about them. Even Silver appeared to sense the atmosphere, placing no further strain on Toni's already overtaxed emotions.

Sliding to the ground, she took off saddle and bridle and turned the animal free before making for the cottage. She could feel Rafe's eyes on her back, but she didn't falter in her step. The sooner she was away from here the better, she told herself fiercely, and knew it wasn't true. She had loved this place, this job, this whole past week. Why, oh, why had Rafe had to come and spoil things?

Another couple of weeks and she would have been gone anyway.

It took her only a little time to pack her suitcase. She had become fond of the cottage. It was a wrench leaving it. When the moment came she went out without a backward glance.

Her car was standing where she had parked it a week ago. After slinging her case in the boot, Toni hesitated. Rafe or no Rafe, she couldn't bring herself to leave without saying goodbye to Sean. None of this was his fault. He was in no way answerable for his brother's bigotry; she had to make that clear to him.

Steeling herself, she went into the lodge, finding Margot busy writing up menus at the lobby desk.

'Is Mr Stewart in there?' she asked, indicating the closed office door behind the girl.

'They both are.' From the sudden embarrassment evidenced in the other's averted eyes, it was apparent that she had some idea of the subject under discussion. The door was mere feet away from her back, and voices tended to carry, especially when raised in anger. Toni could hear one now, although not the actual words. Sean, if she were not mistaken. Well, she could put a stop to that, at least.

The door opened before she could reach it, framing the younger brother for a moment in a manner reminiscent of the first time Toni had seen him. His expression, however, was very different. She had never seen him look so determined.

'I was just coming to find you,' he said. 'Come in here, will you, Toni, please. There's something I want to say.'

Rafe was standing over by the window, hands thrust into the pockets of his jeans. The strong features were hard, his mouth set like a trap. Toni quailed inwardly and involuntarily before the look he gave her.

'Come to collect your dues?' he asked.

Sean closed the door abruptly and stood with his back

against it, almost as if to stop Toni from leaving again. 'I told you,' he stated flatly. 'If she goes I go with her!'

'Oh, now wait a minute!' It was Toni who spoke, her tone rising on a note of concern. 'Sean, what are you talking about?'

'What I say.' The determination was still there, increased if anything. 'I won't let you be turned out of a job you've been doing more than ably for a whole week just to satisfy some personal prejudice. If I'm in charge here then my word goes. If I'm not then *I* go!'

In any other circumstances, Toni would have felt like applauding that speech. Right now she wished she were on her way and out of it. She didn't care to look at Rafe, too well aware of what his reaction would be.

'I'm not going to be the cause of any family rift,' she stated firmly. 'I only came to say goodbye.'

'You're not going. I won't let you go!' His voice took on a note of appeal, faint but unmistakable. 'You want to stay, don't you, Toni?'

She could hardly deny it; not without making a complete liar of herself. She tried to sidestep the question. 'It was a temporary job anyway—we both knew that. It's time I was making tracks.'

'No, it isn't. Not until you have to.' His tone firmed again. 'I meant what I said. If you go because of this, I'm coming with you.'

She stared at him helplessly for a long moment, realising he was serious in the threat. He was putting her in a cleft stick. Either she hurt his already wounded pride further by telling him without equivocation that she didn't want him with her, or she stood with him against his brother in a fight for which she had little stomach.

Her glance towards the latter held a quality halfway between defiance and resignation. 'You'd better tell him the real reason you're getting rid of me. That might convince him how right you are.'

'All on one throw?' The grey eyes were cold enough to freeze. '*You* tell him. I'd like to hear your version myself.'

'Version of what?' Sean sounded bewildered. 'You're not talking about that episode with the cars, are you?'

Toni shook her head. 'Before that. The family I worked for down in Vancouver was named Shannon.' She ignored his surprised exclamation and went on doggedly, 'I left for personal reasons, I told you both a while back. Well, that was true. They were very personal. I objected to a certain person's assumption that I was going to be prepared to jump into bed with him the moment his wife's back was turned for a couple of days.'

'Clever.' Rafe's tone was sardonically admiring. 'You almost make it sound believable!'

'It is believable.' Sean was quick into the breach, recognising some if not all of the situation. 'Craig's a great guy, but he's always had an eye for other women.'

'Not enough to do much about it without encouragement,' his brother returned. 'He admitted to Diane that he'd been tempted by the offer. That's why he got rid of our little English friend here so sharply.'

'He didn't get rid of me,' Toni said with control. 'I walked out.'

'Making sure you had every cent due to you first, of course.'

'I'd been paid the day before for the previous month. I considered myself entitled to cash the cheque, yes.' She was breathing fast but still in command. 'Look, I don't care whether you believe me or not. I'm simply making sure your brother isn't under any illusion as to why I'm being told to go.' Her smile was for Sean, faint but unwavering. 'Thanks for the support anyway.'

'It still stands.' His tone was firm. 'Even if I believed all that it would still stand.' He looked across at his brother with angry eyes. 'What does it have to do with you anyhow?'

'Enough.' Rafe paused, eyeing the younger man in obvious intolerance. 'You're a bigger fool than I thought.'

'Sean, no!' Toni's cry was synonymous with her move to grasp his arm, staying his own sharp movement towards his brother. 'It isn't worth it.'

'You're right, it isn't.' The grey eyes held hers with scorn in their depths. 'So you stay till Bill gets back.'

Toni brought her chin up sharply. 'I don't want——'

'You'd rather be responsible for a family rift?'

She shook her head with impatience, momentarily forgetting that the subject under discussion was right here in the room with them. 'He didn't mean what he said about coming with me.'

'Oh, yes, he did. And I'd say you know him well enough to be aware of it. There's no way I'm going to let him walk out of here with you, and you know that too. You stay.'

'Toni, please!' Sean was watching her face, recognising the beginning of a refusal trembling on her lips. 'For my sake.'

It was unfair, she thought resentfully. He was putting her under intolerable pressure. Yet she could find room to sympathise with his motives too. He had made a stand, and couldn't back down now without losing all self-respect. If she insisted on leaving he would walk out after her.

'All right,' she said, 'I'll stay.' She forced herself to meet Rafe's gaze, knowing just what she would see there. 'I'll do my best to keep your clients happy, Mr. Stewart. That's the main object, isn't it?'

CHAPTER THREE

SEAN was subdued when he carried her suitcase back to the cottage. Toni felt sorry for him, and angry with herself. She had let herself be drawn into this and now she couldn't get out. Not at least for some time. The only consolation in the whole affair was that Rafe Stewart would not be here to make life even more difficult.

Dumping her case on the divan, Sean said softly, 'I want to thank you for backing me up, Toni. It took an issue like this one to make me realise just how far down I'd let myself be pushed. Rafe won't be doing it again, I can tell you!'

Perhaps he wouldn't have done it in the first place had Sean shown signs of having a mind of his own, came the fleeting thought, swiftly dampened. Not for anything was she going to start finding excuses for Rafe Stewart's attitude. He was beyond excuse.

'Forget it,' she said. 'I'm not very keen on being pushed myself. Of course, your brother believes he has reason enough.'

'I don't see why. Like I said before, it wouldn't be anything to do with him even if it were true.'

Toni smiled a little, wondering if he really were as naïve as all that. 'You must realise what he's worried about. He thinks I might have designs on you next.'

'I wish you had.' The grin lifted his features back to their normal buoyancy. 'Anyway, we won, didn't we?'

Except that the fight had not really been hers, she reflected, but refrained from voicing the thought. Sean was feeling good again, pleased with his strike for freedom. Why drag him down?

'Yes, we won,' she agreed. 'I'd better get the horses

back up to the corral.'

'I'll get somebody else to do that for tonight. You've had enough.' His tone was solicitous. 'See you after supper?'

'In company with your brother?' She shook her head. 'I don't think so, thanks. In fact, the less I see of him the better.'

'I'm feeling a bit the same way at present,' he admitted. 'But Rafe's unlikely to hang around too long. Tomorrow's barbecue again. Maybe we could rig up a speaker and have some dancing. All kinds to suit all comers. Sound good?'

Toni was amused, and not a little impressed. Apparently self-assertion was good for the imagination as well as the soul. 'Sounds very good,' she agreed. 'I'm sure they'll all enjoy it. Do you mind if I ask you to go now, Sean? I'd like to change for supper.'

'Not if you'll promise me first dance. I'll make sure it's something I can do.'

'I promise.' Right then she would have promised almost anything in order to be alone. Sean was right; she had had enough. She needed time to gather herself, to lick her wounds and soothe the hurt. Damn Rafe Stewart! Damn all men! Why couldn't they leave her alone!

She knew why, of course. She had been told often enough. Long supple limbs; smooth curves; hair the colour of thick golden honey and a face like a sexy angel was how Randy had once described her in a light moment. A combination of eyes and mouth, he'd added in laughing explanation of the latter statement: a subtle hint of sensuality which made a man yearn to plumb farther. Craig Shannon had said something similar, if perhaps a little less flamboyantly the night he had come to her room.

Toni quivered, remembering his insistence, the hot clutch of his hands dragging her into his arms. As the father of her three charges and the husband of a woman she admired, she had quite liked him up until that moment, persuading herself that the innuendo in his conversational gambits was a figment of her imagination. Well, she had learned her lesson—first from Randy, and now from Craig Shannon. She would not be taken in again so easily.

Neither of the Stewarts put in an appearance over supper. Toni ate alone and hurriedly, not wishing to be around if and when they did show up. It was getting a little too late for Rafe to be thinking of continuing his journey tonight, but with any luck at all he would be away early in the morning. Either way, she shouldn't have to meet up with him again. That was a relief in itself.

She was back at the cottage before eight with a whole evening stretching ahead. At nine she slipped out to the lake for a last bathe in the gathering dusk, staying close by the bank where the rushes grew down into the water. Normally in an evening she would have taken a bath over at the lodge house around ten before making her way back here to bed, but for tonight that was out. The lake was an adequate if rather less refined substitute.

Back indoors she got into nightdress and wrap and boiled some milk on the little portable stove Sean had thoughtfully provided to make herself a drink of hot chocolate before retiring. She wasn't sleepy yet, and the night was still and warm. It was pleasant sitting out on the step with the mug in her hand watching the moonlight on the water. Providing the lights were off in the room behind her, the bugs left her alone.

The site was settling down for the night, the only sounds of revelry coming from the next cottage down, which was a good two hundred feet away. The party of three, all male and in their twenties, had only arrived today, and had spent every minute of daylight out on the lake fishing. Having seen the cases of beer being carried surreptitiously into the place earlier, Toni could only hope they did not intend spending the greater part of the night carousing. Apart from Saturdays, the general rule was as little noise as possible after eleven. Sensible enough considering that most people who stayed here were either transients with a need for an early start next morning, or simply people who wanted a restful vacation in idyllic surroundings.

They seemed to be quietening down, she noted in relief some moments later. Time she was thinking of turning in too, yet her mind was not composed for sleep. Today had been a bad day all round; tomorrow had to be better. Whatever Rafe Stewart might think of her, she was not going to let it get to her.

He came while she was still sitting there on the step, walking so quietly that she was not aware of his approach until he spoke.

'You're likely to get a chill sitting about like that.'

Toni came jerkily to her feet, drawing the edges of her wrap together with one hand in a gesture instinctively protective.

'I was just about to go in,' she said. 'Goodnight, Mr Stewart.'

'Not so fast.' His tone was low but not soft. 'I want to talk to you.' He paused, looking at her, expression assessing. 'On the other hand, maybe we'd be better doing it indoors.'

Her voice sounded tight. 'Whatever you have to say you can say it out here. Only if it's just a repetition of what you said earlier, you're wasting your time.'

'Not a habit of mine,' he said with meaning. He waited a brief moment, then shrugged broad shoulders. 'So I'll say it out here. How much do you want to get out right now? Tonight.'

Toni gazed at him in total silence for a long, long moment, this tall, lean man with the granite features and a matching heart. Her first instinct was to hit him, but some other part of her took over instead, controlling both face and voice in a manner which amazed her in retrospect.

'How much are you offering?'

The faint curl of his upper lip was the only indication he gave. 'I can give you a thousand in cash. That's all I can get together. There'll be a draft for another thousand to go with it.'

'Which you could have stopped the minute the banks open for business,' she pointed out, still in the same cool tones.

'Hardly worth my while,' he said. ''Cause too much speculation in the wrong quarters. You have my word on that.'

'As a man of honour?' She let the irony stand in her eyes as well as her voice, registering the thinning of his lips with a certain satisfaction. The extension of her open palm was equally calculated. 'Give me the money.'

The roll of bills he took from a back pocket looked thick. 'They're mostly small,' he said, placing it in her hand. 'Petty cash. Want to count it?'

'I don't think that will be necessary, thanks.' Toni slipped off the rubber band holding the notes, and straightened them out between both hands. Anger lent her the strength she needed. '*This* is what I think of your offer!' she said between her teeth.

Rafe made no move to pick up the torn halves of banknotes littering both step and grass where she had dropped them. The grey eyes held a dangerous glitter.

'Playing for higher stakes?' he asked.

She was suddenly sickened by the whole affair; not least ashamed of her own part in it these last few moments.

'I'm not leaving,' she stated flatly. 'You can think what you like, but I'm not going to be driven out! Now, if you don't mind, I'd like to go to bed.'

'I'll accommodate you.'

He was up the step even as she turned away, pushing

her ahead of him through the open door and closing it behind him. Too frozen by shock to put up any real resistance, Toni felt herself lifted and carried. Then she was on the bed and his weight was pinning her, his hands clamping her wrists so that she couldn't get her fingers to his face.

'This is what you don't like, isn't it?' he said roughly. 'Having control taken away from you! Craig told me about that. He told me everything! He still isn't over what you did to him, you little bitch!'

'I didn't do anything!' She was frightened but not cowed, her whole body tensed in rejection. 'Whatever he told you it isn't true!'

'Isn't it?' His mouth was a straight taut line, the words clipped out with scarcely a movement of his lips. 'Not the way you encouraged him for weeks until he couldn't hold out any longer?'

'No!'

'You're a liar! You thought you could play him like a fish until you had him netted. And then what? A word in Diane's ear? Or maybe just the threat of it? Only he came on too fast for you, didn't he? He wanted too much too soon. You should have gone along with him. The end would have been the same—Diane would leave him like a shot if she ever had confirmation he'd been unfaithful with you. You might even have been in with a chance!'

'It wasn't like that.' She was appealing now, trying to make him see. 'He's twisted the whole thing round!'

'Like hell he has!' The laugh grated. 'I've seen the effect you've had on Sean in just a week. He's hardly the type to read too much into too little.'

'But he's the type to react pretty strongly if he knew about this,' Toni came back, giving up the unequal battle. He wasn't going to believe her, not if she argued her case for a hundred years! 'Would you really like him to know he has a common rapist for a brother? Because that's what you'll have to do.'

For a horrible moment she thought she had overplayed her hand as Rafe's face visibly hardened. With some deliberation he ran his eyes down the full length of her body, lingering on the slender lines of her legs, outlined by the tautly pulled material of her nightdress.

'It might almost be worth it,' he said, 'just to put you down.' He looked at her for another long moment, contempt in his eyes, then abruptly released her. 'You'll get what's coming to you one of these days. Leave Sean alone, do you hear!'

Toni was silent, not trusting herself to speak. Her wrists hurt from the pressure of his fingers, but the pain was as nothing compared with the anger inside her. He hadn't given her a chance; not one solitary chance! Cold common sense told her that the best course of action was to get out now and leave the two brothers to sort out their own differences, but pride wouldn't allow her to crawl away in the night like someone who really was guilty of all the things he had accused her of. She had promised Sean she would stay on until Bill came back, and that was what she was going to do, no matter how uncomfortable Rafe Stewart tried to make her life.

It was something of an anti-climax to find Rafe had already left when she went over for breakfast next morning. Somehow she hadn't expected him to give up as easily as that. Sean was cock-a-hoop, believing himself the outright winner of this particular family altercation. Toni made no attempt to pull him down from his pedestal. He needed a little more confidence in himself.

The weekend passed pleasantly, its highlight the Saturday night barbecue. True to his word, Sean had an extension speaker rigged up to provide music for dancing on a flat stretch of grass close by the barbecue pits, starting off with a beat number for which he claimed

Toni as his partner.

'I'm saving the more romantic stuff for later on when it's dark,' he grinned. 'By which time I'll be free to do them all with you. Don't forget you're booked!'

Toni made some light reply and a mental reservation, helped out in the latter instance by the combined attentions of the three young men who occupied the cottage next to hers. All around Sean's age, they proved to be excellent entertainment for the whole gathering, at one time producing guitars and treating them to an impromptu concert of country and Western songs which had everyone joining in.

Seated between one of the players and the mother of two of her riding pupils, Toni pretended not to see Sean's signals indicating the spare seat on the log beside him. While doubting that his interest in her was anything more than light and passing, she saw no harm in refusing to allow him to monopolise her, especially in the light of one or two comments made this evening on that very subject. If other people had noted how much time they had spent together then it was certainly more than time to do something about it. At least her conscience would be clear should Rafe Stewart put in any further appearance before she finally left.

It wasn't as simple as that, of course, because Sean himself wouldn't allow it to be. In the absence, however, of any attempt to put their relationship on anything but a friendly footing, Toni decided that she herself had been reading too much into too little and relaxed her guard. She enjoyed Sean's company and he enjoyed hers. What harm could there be in that?

She had become friendly too with the three in the next cottage, finding quite a lot in common with the one named Mike, who at twenty-five was the eldest of the trio, and the only one willing to take time off from fishing during the day in order to ride. The three of them had been friends since high school, he told her on one occasion. They had been coming to Copper Lake as a group for three years now, and were favourably impressed by the new management.

'There's more going on,' he said. 'More people here. Food's good too. Two weeks of little else but fish can get a bit monotonous.'

'I'd have thought the three of you were a bit young to spend a whole two weeks' vacation just fishing,' Toni commented lightly, and he laughed.

'Something only another fisherman would understand. I picked it up from my father when I was a kid. Guess Bobby and Clint did the same. Anyway, we all take another vacation later on and do our own thing.' He paused, pale blue eyes glancing sideways. 'You going to be here all season?'

Toni shook her head, feeling a pang of regret. 'Only until the regular rider gets back. That should be this weekend.'

It was Thursday when Sean gave her the news.

'Bill can't make it for at least another week, maybe two,' he said, trying to hide a certain jubilation. 'It's his daughter. Apparently she's going through a marital crisis and he doesn't feel able to opt out and leave his wife to it all. You can stay on, can't you?'

Toni hesitated, not at all sure that she should even consider it. Yet if she went she would be leaving Sean in the same lurch. The riding facility was so popular. Many would be the long face if it were taken away, and that was hardly good for business. And where was the problem really? She and Sean had a healthy, well-balanced relationship with no misconceptions. Two weeks or four—what difference would it make?

'Yes,' she said, 'I can stay. I'm not sure how your brother's going to feel about it, though.'

'It isn't his concern.' Sean's whole face was lit. 'If this

had to happen to Bill at all I'm sure glad it happened now. You don't know what a difference you've made to the place, Toni.'

She was popular; it would have been false modesty to deny it. She laughed instead and shook her head. 'I'm sure Bill had his following too. Can't hang about—I'm due out again in five minutes. See you later.'

Despite what Sean had said, she found herself wondering just what Rafe Stewart's reaction would be. Already he had stretched a point in leaving her here without supervision. How would he feel about another two weeks?

Rough, she was willing to bet. But enough so to make another attempt at persuading Sean to get rid of her? She doubted it. The latter had stood up to him once and would do it again; Rafe must realise that. No, he might fume and chafe, but there was little he could do about it. Sean had him over a barrel.

It appeared she was right in her assessment as the weekend passed and another week got under way. Rafe had given up. Always providing Sean had told him, that was. Yet Toni refused to believe he would deliberately have lied about it. The whole affair was his one big triumph. More likely he would be only too ready to flaunt it in his brother's face.

Friday was a busy day. With most of the cottages and sites changing clientele in the morning, almost everyone who had sat a horse at all that week wanted a last ride before going home. Riding Silver on an almost permanent basis now, Toni was able to take out five at a time, although still insisting that the horses had at least half an hour to rest and graze between each ride. It was gone seven before she finally corralled the string.

Too late now to go and change before supper, she decided tiredly. A quick wash and brush up in one of the bathrooms would have to suffice. Sean often joined her for coffee even if he had already eaten himself, but tonight there was no sign of him. He could have gone into town, of course.

It was one of the waitresses who eventually told her where he was. Rafe Stewart had come in about an hour ago while Toni was still out on that last ride. He'd brought a bag with him and taken over a room, so it looked as if he might be planning on staying a few days this time, she added chattily while waiting for Toni to sign her chit. He and Sean were in the back right now.

Making her way to the cottage, Toni wondered depressedly how long it would be before she received another visit from the elder Stewart brother. The last thing she felt like tonight was another battle royal.

On the other hand, why should there be one? she comforted herself. If Rafe had intended any further action he would have put in an appearance before this. He might be taking an opportunity to check up on her, but there was nothing he would find against her this time. Sean would put him right on that score. They were friends, nothing else.

Mike came over around nine to ask her to join a party of the younger folk for a last get-together, accepting her plea of tiredness with good grace.

'Maybe we'll meet up in Calgary at the Stampede,' he said. 'You should have finished here by then. It's a great time of year. Being a rider yourself you'd enjoy it all the more.'

The party was loud and riotous and showed little sign of quieting down when eleven came and went. By midnight, Toni could stand it no longer. She hated to be a spoilsport, but enough was really enough. Sleep was impossible while that racket was going on.

She dressed swiftly in jeans and shirt before going over to the other cottage—an act for which she was to be grateful later on. Mike opened the door to her knock, a glass in his hand and an ear-to-ear grin splitting his face.

'Well, lookit who's here!' he exclaimed on a decidedly inebriated note. 'Change your mind, did you, hon? Better late than never. Come and have a drink.'

Toni shook her head, trying not to sound censorious about it. 'I came to ask if you could tone things down a bit. It's awfully late.'

'Hey, you guys!' Mike turned with an exaggerated movement of a finger to his lips. 'Keep it down, will you! Folks wanna sleep.'

There was no appreciable decrease in the sounds issuing from within; Toni doubted if anyone had even heard the plea. Catching Mike's wryly humorous shrug, she sighed and acknowledged defeat. The only thing likely to stop proceedings on a voluntary basis was a simple lack of will to carry on, and that might not be for hours yet. Where were the Stewarts anyway? It was surely their place to put an end to the disturbance, considering the rules were theirs to begin with!

Rafe's sudden appearance seemed almost in direct response to her question. He came up the step behind her, moving her to one side to step past the man in the doorway and into the room beyond. An instant later the blare of music ceased abruptly, to be replaced by an indignant clamour of voices.

'That's it,' Toni heard him state. 'Everybody out. And I mean *now*!'

They came filing past like sheep, one or two muttering imprecations but no one actually prepared to stay and argue about it. Mike watched them go with a comical look of uncertainty on his face, as if not quite understanding why the party had so suddenly finished.

Rafe came last, his glance skimming briefly over Toni as he turned his head to the younger man. 'Your friends are sleeping it off. I'd suggest you do the same. And if you come here again leave the liquor at home, okay?'

Mike nodded, gave Toni a feeble attempt at a

nonchalant wave, and vanished indoors, closing the door behind him.

Meeting the grey gaze now turned fully on her, Toni forced herself to stand her ground. She had not been a party to what had been going on in there, and there was no way he was going to tie her in.

'If you'd done that an hour ago we might all be asleep by now,' she said shortly. 'The rule is eleven, isn't it?'

'Most times, yes.' He sounded surprisingly mild. 'I gave them as much leeway as I could, considering. I gather you came over to complain yourself.'

'For what good it did me.' She was silent for a moment, unable to comprehend the difference in his attitude from their last meeting. Her next words were almost in challenge of that difference. 'Where's Sean?'

There was no appreciable change in his expression. 'I told him I'd handle it. Come on, I'll walk you back to your cottage.'

'It's only next door,' she pointed out with a lift of her chin. 'And I'd rather go alone, thanks.'

'I can't say I blame you all that much.' The note was rueful now. 'I gave you a rough time, didn't I? I'm not making excuses. I really thought you had it coming.'

Toni stared at him in the semi-darkness, hardly able to credit what her senses seemed to be telling her. 'And now?' she prompted at last, and heard the unsteadiness of her voice without surprise.

'I've had time to think things over,' he said. 'Time to realise I might have been a bit too hasty in putting all the blame on you. Craig probably made the running initially, which——'

'Craig made all the running,' she cut in with determination. 'If you're not prepared to believe that then I'm not interested in hearing any more.'

His eyes narrowed fractionally as he studied her, then his shoulders lifted. 'Okay, so he lied to save his marriage.

That's understandable, I guess, Diane being who she is.'

'He wouldn't have had to bother if he'd stayed away from me in the first place,' Toni said. 'I lost a good job because of him!'

'But you found another. Not quite the same, of course, but it has its compensations.'

She looked at him suspiciously. 'Meaning Sean?'

'Meaning more freedom. Sean's too young for you. I should have realised that too.'

'Except that it wasn't his age you thought I might be interested in,' she came back pointedly, and received another of the rueful smiles.

'Not any more. You're smart enough to have realised by now that Sean doesn't come into his own for another two years, and yet you're still here.' He paused a moment, eyes lacking in the coldness she had come to expect from him. 'What I'm trying to say is, how about starting over? Forget the whole thing?'

Warmth was rising in her, curling up from somewhere deep down inside as if too long held in. 'Even my driving?' she heard herself ask on a purposely light note, and he smiled again, this time with humour.

'I take back nothing I said that time. I was a first-hand witness, remember?'

'And I was a day-dreaming idiot,' she conceded. 'For the record, my mind will be strictly on the road in future.'

'I'm glad to hear it.' Rafe indicated the smaller cottage with a brief inclination of his head. 'Going to trust me now?'

It still seemed unecessary considering how close they were, but something in her wanted it anyway. She had never felt quite so supremely aware of a man as she did at this moment.

'Are you planning on staying over the weekend?' she asked as they moved side by side along the pathway between the two dwellings.

'More than that,' he said. 'I'm taking over from Sean for a few days while he goes on home. His mother wants to see him, and she doesn't feel equal to coming out here.'

Toni turned her head, struck by a certain inflection in his voice 'Is she ill?'

'She was made a paraplegic in the car crash which killed my father.' It was said matter-of-factly. 'She gets around fine by wheelchair and a specially equipped car at home, but longer journeys are tiring for her.'

'I'm sorry.' Toni wished she could find some less inadequate way of expressing her sympathy. 'Sean never told me about that.'

'Maybe he just didn't get around to it yet.' They had reached the other cottage, and Rafe came to a halt at the foot of the two shallow steps, a hand on the rail. The moonlight lent a certain hardness to the line of his mouth. Then he smiled and the hardness was gone. 'What time do you get through tomorrow?'

She was surprised, not quite comprehending. 'It depends on bookings.'

'You should make yourself a deadline for the last ride of the day,' he came back. 'Say five. That would mean you'd have the horses corralled for the night by six-thirty. Dinner at eight?'

'Here?'

He laughed and shook his head. 'I think we can do a bit better than that. There's a place called Pine Lodge some way north-west of here. It's a bit off the beaten track, but what they can do with Lake trout makes it more than worthwhile. Anyway, it would be a change for you. Sean tells me you haven't been off the place in three weeks!'

'I haven't felt any need,' Toni admitted. She paused there, feeling her way. 'You don't have to feel obligated because of—last time. It's enough that you believe me.'

'Is it?' His tone was odd. 'Well, I'd still like to take you to dinner. Okay?'

'Okay.' Toni felt suddenly and overwhelmingly light-hearted, her smile spontaneous in its warmth. 'I'd like that too, Rafe.'

'Good.' He made no attempt to touch her, inclining his head in the direction of the door. 'I'll watch you in. And lock it after you. Our friends over there might take it into their heads to do a spot of sleepwalking.' He paused consideringly. 'Maybe we should think about moving you over to the main building.'

'I've never had any trouble,' she protested. 'And I'd rather be out here.'

'Privacy does have its advantages,' he agreed. 'All right, it's up to you.' He smiled again, voice softening. 'Goodnight, Toni.'

On his lips her name sounded different. Or was it just, Toni wondered as she closed the door between them, that she found him so different? Only two weeks ago Rafe had tossed her down on that bed over there and accused her of trying to ruin his friend's marriage, and now here he was asking her out. It took a big man to admit he could be so wrong. One had to admire him for it.

There was more to it than that, she acknowledged with a wry little smile. She was attracted to Rafe Stewart, and had been from the first moment of meeting, despite everything that had passed between them. What she had to guard against now was letting the barriers drop too far. It would be fatally easy to like this new Rafe too much.

CHAPTER FOUR

SEAN was on the point of leaving when Toni came out after breakfast. He was driving through to Calgary in the one hop, he told her. He seemed singularly lacking in enthusiasm for the whole trip.

'You're going to be here when I get back, aren't you?' he asked on an urgent note. 'I mean, you wouldn't just go?'

'Of course not,' she said. 'You're only going to be away a few days.'

The hesitancy vanished, replaced by a smile. 'That's all I need to know. Take care of yourself, Toni. I'd hate anything to happen to you. And don't let that brother of mine worry you either.'

There was more to that last injunction than he knew, Toni thought wryly, watching the car move off up the lane. Rafe had been on her mind since waking this morning. Turning now to find the subject of her thoughts watching her from the lobby doorway, she felt the colour faintly touch her cheeks. She found herself searching his face for some sign of last night's gentler mood.

His smile was reassuring. No more hostilities, it seemed to say; we're going to be friends. 'Did you eat yet?' he asked.

Toni nodded. 'I was just going up to fetch the horses. It's going to be a busy day.'

'Then I won't keep you. I thought we'd leave about a quarter after seven. That suit?'

'Lovely.' It was all she could think of to say. She had never felt tongue-tied with a man before, but she did with this one. Perhaps because of what had gone before—or was it simply that she couldn't quite fathom out what was to come? There had been no real necessity for anyone to stand in for Sean. Not for a few days. Which meant Rafe had elected to stay. Because of her? She wished she could be sure. It was suddenly very important to know.

She didn't see him again all day. Corralling the horses at six-thirty, she found herself looking forward to the evening with a sharp anticipation in no way tempered by memories of past encounters. For the first time she regretted the lack of bathroom facilities that necessitated taking along her things to the Lodge house in order to shower and change. It meant leaving her soiled clothing there for the evening as she had neither time nor inclination to make the journey back to the cottage before meeting Rafe.

Eager to get away from the jeans and shirt image he must have of her, she had chosen to wear a simple shirtwaist in a pale green which offset her hair and growing tan to the best advantage. Rafe was waiting for her in the lobby when she went down, a light, casual jacket over his open-necked shirt and toning slacks. There was no mistaking the frank appreciation in his eyes as he looked at her.

'I don't wonder Craig went overboard,' he said softly when he was putting her into the convertible.

There was no irony in the statement, nor any apparent in the grey eyes when she looked up at him swiftly, yet the sting was there, even if only in her own mind.

'I thought we were going to forget about that?' she said.

'So we are.' He slid behind the wheel, smiling at her in a way that would have made her forgive him almost anything. 'There are other things to think about.'

Pine Lodge was far enough off the beaten track to discourage casual trade, yet well enough known to maintain a regular clientele. The view from the west-facing restaurant was tremendous. Toni felt she could have sat there for ever just drinking it in.

'The Rockies are full of scenes like this one,' said Rafe when she tried to communicate something of her impressions over coffee. 'I'm not saying it palls, but after a time it becomes accepted.' The pause was just long enough. 'I'm more interested in the view right across the table.'

Green eyes lifted to meet grey, reflecting the smile which moved her lips. 'Why?' she asked.

For a brief moment he looked taken aback, then he laughed and shook his head. 'You know why. We both do. It happened the very first time we met right out there on the highway.'

'You didn't give that impression.' Toni kept her tone light. 'Anything but.'

'I was trying not to let the look of you impair my judgement,' he admitted dryly. 'Could be I went too far the other way.' He paused, eyes holding hers. 'I took your number with the intention of trying to trace you later. You were heading east; there seemed a fair chance you'd be making for Calgary.' The smile took on a wry quality. 'Then Diane showed me that photograph of you with the kids and the whole idea went sour on me. Coming back here and finding you with Sean wound round your little finger was like waving a red rag in front of a bull. I knew damn well what Craig was like, but I wouldn't let myself believe it.'

Her voice sounded husky. 'What changed your mind?'

'I told you. Once I gave myself time to think about it I realised I'd been unfair to you—and to myself. This trip of Sean's seemed an ideal opportunity to make my peace.' One dark eyebrow quirked. 'How am I doing so far?'

'Admirably.' Toni was trying not to show how his words were affecting her. 'Sean seemed to think his journey wasn't really necessary.'

'It was.' There was a quiet certainty in the statement. 'Karen wants to see her son. That makes it necessary.' He watched the faint drawing together of her brows and shook his head. 'My mother died when I was eight and my father married again within the. year. Sean was born the year after.'

'And you've never felt able to call her mother yourself?'

Broad shoulders lifted briefly. 'She's only ten years older than me. It was more like acquiring an older sister. My father was only in his mid-thirties, so the difference wasn't so great.'

'You resented her?' The question was soft, drawing a sudden bright gleam of amusement to the grey eyes.

'No, I resented my father for coming between us. She was everything a nine-year-old boy could want in a companion—old enough to open doors he couldn't open but not too old to come down to his level when the occasion called for it. I'd have done anything for her.' The amusement faded a little, shadowed by some other emotion not as easily defined. 'I still would. Fifteen years in a wheelchair would make a lot of women emotional as well as physical cripples, but not Karen. She's the most courageous person I know.'

Analysing her initial instinctive response, Toni came to the conclusion that it was envy rather than jealousy which had prompted the quick stab. For a fleeting moment she had wished herself the recipient of such admiration. Yet what a price to pay for the privilege! Karen Stewart could only have been in her late twenties when the accident had happened. It took more than courage to come through the loss of both husband and mobility without bitterness; it took an indomitable spirit.

'She must be an exceptional woman,' she said.

'She is.' It was a simple statement of fact. Then his tone lightened. 'Tell me about yourself. What made you come to Canada in the first place?'

That was one question Toni did not want to answer in full. The hurt Randy had inflicted had not gone as deep as she had thought, true enough, but it was not a subject she cared to discuss with another man. She compromised instead.

'I was offered a job that didn't turn out to be quite what I'd hoped. Working for the Shannons was just meant to be a stopgap until I found something else.'

'And when you leave here?' The tone was still light.

'It depends,' she said, thinking ahead to the day when she would be alone again without enthusiasm. 'I'm not sure how things might work out yet.'

'No, I guess not.' He held up a hand to the waitress for the check, eyes coming back to her face with an expression that quickened her heartbeats. 'We'll have to talk about it.'

Toni was quiet in the car going back towards Copper Lake, trying to come to terms with her own emotional instability. She had thought herself in love with Randy a bare two months ago, now here she was as strongly, if not more so, attracted to another man she barely knew. And what of Rafe himself? How serious was he in what he had said tonight? He could be giving her the rush in the hope of a quick conquest, of course, but she somehow didn't think so. It took more than that to make a man like Rafe sacrifice whole days of his time.

They were home before eleven, finding the barbecue crowd already dispersed by the cool breeze blowing off the water.

'Sean ran an extension for dancing out here the last two weekends,' Toni commented as they got out of the car. 'I suppose nobody thought of it this week when he's away. It seemed a great success.'

'I'm sure it was.' Rafe sounded surprised, as if the notion of his brother having good ideas went beyond his experience. 'He should make it a permanent arrangement.' He paused, glancing down at her, face hard-boned in the moonlight. 'How about a nightcap?'

'I should be going,' she hedged, not really wanting the evening to end so soon, yet conscious too of a need to be on her own away from his disturbing influence. 'I promised a couple of the children I'd take them out before breakfast.'

'It isn't late,' he said, 'and I'd appreciate your company.'

'You've had it all evening,' she pointed out, and drew a smile.

'A little more of it, then. I'm your boss. Shall I make it an order?'

Her laugh signified capitulation. 'Strictly speaking it's outside your province, but we won't argue about it. Lead the way.'

Sean's small sitting room seemed even smaller with the curtains drawn and only the light from a couple of lamps to illuminate it. Seating herself on the smaller of the two settees, Toni watched Rafe pour the Grand Marnier she had requested along with a Scotch for himself and bring the two glasses across.

'What made you decide to go into this sort of thing?' she asked, taking hers from him. 'It hardly seems the kind of business a company like yours would be interested in.'

'On this scale, no, it isn't,' he admitted, taking a seat next to her. 'Copper Lake's just a try-out. If the end of the season shows a good enough picture, we'll be opening up a chain across the country under the same general plan, running motel and campsite together.'

'With Sean in charge?'

'If he shows himself capable.'

'He seems to be doing that here.'

'There's a difference between running one place and organising a dozen. So far his record isn't outstanding.'

'He's only twenty-three,' Toni protested. 'He's still finding his feet. Just because you knew what you wanted at that age it doesn't necessarily have to follow that Sean has to be the same.' She stopped there, aware that none of this was her concern and suddenly appalled at her temerity. 'I'm sorry,' she began, 'I——'

Rafe was looking down at the glass in his hand with an unreadable expression. 'What makes you so sure I knew what I wanted at Sean's age?'

'Instinct.' She was on firmer ground here. 'I think you've probably always known just what you wanted, Rafe.'

'You could be right.' His move to put down the glass on the lamp table at his side was slow and purposeful. 'Like now.'

Toni relinquished her own glass without protest, knowing what was going to happen and wanting it too. The last time he had kissed her he had been brutal about it, this time he did it with finesse, the movement of his lips slow and sensuous against hers. Toni responded instinctively, mouth soft and yielding, her body curving into the circle of his arms. She could feel the hardness of his chest against her breasts, the ripple of muscle beneath her fingers. There was strength in those broad shoulders, tempered now but ready for use. She had felt that strength the night he had carried her into the cottage and laid her on the bed; had known then that resistance was futile. Tonight she didn't want to resist.

Rafe was the first to pull up, lifting his head to look at her without letting her go. The grey eyes had lost their coolness. When he spoke it was with a roughness he made no attempt to conceal.

'Are you always so quick to arousal, or can I flatter myself I'm a special case?'

She reached up a hand to touch his face, shaken by the intensity of her emotions. 'You're a very special case,' she whispered thickly. 'I never felt like this before, Rafe. Not even close.'

'Tell me how you feel.' The demand came low. 'What

makes me different from the others?'

'There haven't been any others,' she said. 'Not the way you mean.'

'You mean you've been saving yourself for someone like me?'

The irony brought warmth to her face. Abruptly she pushed herself away from him. 'If that's what you think there's no point in talking!'

Rafe reached for her as she got to her feet, drawing her down again and holding her there. 'Don't run away. It was a nasty crack, and unnecessary.'

Toni relaxed a little, but only a little, searching the lean, intelligent features without success. It was impossible to read the mind behind the grey eyes, to guess what he was really thinking. 'You're still not wholly convinced about Craig Shannon, are you?' she said. 'You still believe I must have encouraged him.'

'To a certain extent,' he admitted. 'Maybe without even realising it.'

'It must have been.' Her tone was bitter. 'If I have to stop and consider every little thing I say or do for possible misinterpretation I'm not going to get very far.'

'But it might save you a lot of hassle in the long run.' One hand slid under her hair, holding the back of her neck in a clasp just firm enough to keep her still. His eyes were on her mouth, the look in them making her quiver. 'Right now I'm not misinterpreting anything. You want me to make love to you as much as I want to do it.'

Toni made no attempt to deny it; the knowledge was an ache inside her. She only wished herself capable of indulging that need with detachment from other emotions, the way Rafe obviously was.

'What I want doesn't make any difference,' she said. 'It isn't going to happen.'

'Why not?' The hand was moving, the ball of his thumb caressing her nape with a touch that set her alight, his other hand warm on her skin as he slid it so very gently down her arm. 'You'd enjoy it, I'd make sure of that. We'd both enjoy it.'

She closed her eyes at the touch of his hand on her breast, fighting the desire to abandon herself wholly to this one moment and be damned to the rest. Rafe would be an expert lover; the kind one dreamed about. She believed him when he said he would make her enjoy it. What he was doing to her now went beyond mere gratification.

It took every ounce of willpower she had to pull that hand away from her. She said fiercely, 'This is one time you're not going to have your own way, Rafe. It's so easy for you, isn't it? Take what you can get and to hell with everything else! Well, not with me you don't. I don't live that way!'

'Okay!' He was angry himself now, letting her go with abruptness. 'Just cool it, will you? If it's no, it's no. You don't have to take a stick and beat it into me!'

She was already regretting the outburst. Instinctively she found herself trying to justify it. 'I just don't like being taken for granted, that's all.'

'I took nothing for granted.' His tone was harsh. 'I was following a natural impulse which appeared to be shared up until a few moments ago.'

'We hardly know one another,' she protested weakly, and saw his lips twist.

'There's nobody could be *that* naïve.'

She flushed, accepting the implication because she knew it was deserved. 'All right, so it happens. To you it probably happens all the time!'

'Not all the time,' he came back with irony. 'Tonight I met the immovable object. Who *are* you saving it for?'

She looked at him for a long moment, not bothering to keep the disgust from her eyes. When she got to her feet her limbs felt amazingly steady. 'Goodnight, Mr Stewart.'

'Toni.' His voice caught her at the door, stopping her despite herself. 'Wait a minute—please.'

It was the last which brought her head round. Rafe Stewart was not a man to whom that word came easily. He was sitting where she had left him, but on the edge of the cushion as if about to rise. The expression on his face was hard to decipher.

'Come on back here,' he said. 'I won't touch you, I just want to talk.'

Toni didn't move. 'Whatever you have to say can be said from there.'

'All right.' He sounded resigned, and more than a little rueful. 'I apologise. I had you wrong. At the risk of repeating myself once too often, can we give it another go?'

She hesitated, disarmed yet still not fully trusting. 'To what purpose?' she asked at last.

His smile was fleeting. 'Who knows? All I do know is what you do to me. Did you ever hear that old song "I've Got You Under My Skin"? That's the way I feel.'

Her own smile was slow. 'It sounds irritating.'

'It is—painfully. I'd like a chance to work it out.' He held up a quick hand. 'Your pace. That's a promise.'

'Sean will be back in a few days,' she reminded him softly, 'and you'll be gone. What's the use?'

'I'm only half an hour from here by air,' he came back. 'And my own boss. You said we hardly knew one another. I'd like to remedy that for a start. When Bill shows up again you could come on through to town and I'll take you around. By that time we'll be in a position to know how we both feel.'

Right now she felt bemused. Not five minutes ago he had been intent on only one aspect of a relationship, here he seemed to be planning a whole possible future. Yet she had to believe he meant what he said. There was no point in it otherwise. She wanted to believe it; she had never wanted anything as much in her life.

Her voice sounded husky. 'All right, I'd like that too.'

'Good.' Rafe came to his feet, lean, lithe and so totally unpredictable, shaking his head as he saw her expression change. 'I'm going to see you back to your cabin, nothing more. And don't say you can see yourself back, because that might suggest a lack of trust in my word.'

'I wasn't arguing,' she said.

He didn't touch her on the way across to the cottage, walking at her side with an easy stride scaled down a little to accommodate her own. The breeze was stronger, coming in sharp gusts. For the first time since her arrival here cloud was obscuring the sky, blotting out the stars from the south.

'Might be in for a storm later on,' Rafe observed when they reached the steps. 'Don't let it alarm you. The sound effects can be pretty spectacular, but you'll be safe enough inside.'

'I'm not afraid of storms,' Toni assured him. She looked at him uncertainly, not quite sure how he intended taking his leave. From the ironic curve of his lips he knew only too well what she was thinking.

'Try shaking hands,' he suggested. 'That shouldn't cause any complications.'

Her breath came out on a sigh. 'Don't make fun of me, Rafe. I can't help the way I am.'

'Neither can I.' He paused, studying her, eyes veiled by something only he could be sure of. 'So we'll start at square one again,' he said. 'Something like this.'

The kiss was over quickly; too quickly. It left her yearning, the way it had been intended to. Then he was gone, striding away over the grass without a backward glance; a man she hadn't even begun to understand.

Bill's return on the Tuesday came as a complete surprise to everyone. A quiet, almost taciturn man in his late fifties, he spent a brief few minutes with Rafe in the office, then came right out to where Toni was saddling up Silver ready for the next ride.

'I hear you've been doing a good job,' he said gruffly. 'Thanks for standing in. The boss wants to see you.'

She found Rafe in the office going through the books. 'I seem to be redundant,' she said wryly. 'Unless you can find me something else to do for the next few days. I promised Sean I'd wait till he got back.'

Something flickered in the grey eyes looking up at her. 'You don't have to do anything. You deserve a rest. With Sherwood back we could both take a day off and fly across to Kamloops. Sound good?'

'Very.' She smiled at him, aware, as always, of the stirring of her senses. 'But can you afford the time?'

'For you?' He put down his pen, standing up to stretch out an inviting hand. 'Come over here.'

Toni went unhesitatingly, lifting her mouth to his with a response she couldn't and didn't try to conceal. In three days they had moved quite a long way from square one, but only as far and as fast as she had wanted to go. Today Rafe showed the first sign of taking over the pace again, holding her to him with an intimacy that made her pulses race.

'You've got me tied up in knots,' he murmured against her hair. 'You know it too. We're going to make the most of these next couple of days until Sean gets back. And after that——' he left the sentence unfinished, the promise there in the possessive clasp of his hands about her slim hips, the growing demand in his lips.

It was a promise repeated many times over those two days, one to which Toni could only respond blindly. Compared with this, she knew her feelings for Randy had been like water to wine. She was intoxicated—too far gone to sit back and view the situation with any degree of objectivity. All she wanted was to be with Rafe, to talk to him, to have his hands hold her close and feel his mouth on hers—that strong, chiselled, wonderful mouth which could lift her to another plane of emotion.

They were flying back from Kamloops on the Thursday afternoon when she acknowledged to herself that she was in love with him. It had happened so fast she could scarcely believe it, yet it was true just the same. Watching Rafe's hands so sure on the controls, she wondered how deeply he really felt about her. That he wanted her he had demonstrated on many occasions, that he enjoyed her company she was willing to accept; it was only when it came to his emotional involvement that the doubts began to creep in.

His smile as he glanced round and caught her watching him served to offer some reassurance. 'Enjoying it?'

Toni nodded, smiling back. 'I never thought I'd feel safe in a plane this size,' she said, 'but I haven't had one queasy moment. How long have you been flying?'

'I got my licence when I was twenty.' Just for a moment a cloud seemed to pass over the grey eyes. 'I prefer it to driving. We'll be landing in a few minutes.'

His mood had changed subtly, and Toni wondered why. She could find nothing in what either of them had said to elicit that faint contraction of his jaw muscles. Some memory conjured up by that reference to his younger days, perhaps? Something he hadn't liked re-membering. Toni contemplated asking, then swiftly rejected the thought. What was past was past and should remain there. In any case, she doubted if he would be willing to tell her.

The landing was uneventful. Jumping down from the step with Rafe's aid, Toni felt moved to put her lips to his in a brief but stimulating salute.

'That's for today,' she said. 'And all the other days. It's been wonderful!'

'Nothing's over,' he returned with an odd inflection.

'There's more to come—if you want it.'

If she wanted it! She looked at him with her heart in her eyes. 'Of course I do. Can you doubt it?'

Rafe shook his head, mouth tilting. 'Do you want to go up to Pine again tonight, or would you rather stay on here?'

'Oh, let's stay here,' she came back impulsively. 'We could go for a swim later on. The water's wonderful at night!'

'Sounds good,' he agreed.

Margot was on reception filling in some forms. She looked up on their entry, glance flicking speculatively from one to the other before finally fixing on Rafe.

'Mrs Stewart phoned earlier. She asked for you to phone her back the minute you got in. She said it was vital.'

'Did she?' Rafe's tone revealed little. He looked at Toni and lifted his shoulders in apology. 'Guess I'd better go and do it. See you at supper.'

Supper was more than an hour away. How long, she wondered, did a simple phone call take? She was immediately ashamed of the thought. She had been in Rafe's company all day; surely she could hardly begrudge his stepmother a little time. She smiled and nodded.

'Fine.'

Making her way across to the cottage she pondered on the possible reasons behind the call. Business in all probability, yet there had been something in Rafe's demeanour which suggested otherwise. Not for the first time she found herself dwelling on the relationship between Karen Stewart and her stepson. With only ten years separating them, it seemed somehow incongruous to think in terms of that particular relationship at all. More like an older sister, Rafe had said, but that had been when he was a child. How did he regard her now?

With admiration, that was obvious; with solicitousness,

that was also obvious. With affection? Toni wasn't at all sure. Tenderness was not an emotion that came easily to a man like Rafe; she had yet to experience it in him herself. Perhaps Karen had no need of it anyway, but that she wouldn't know without meeting her. Somehow that prospect held little appeal.

CHAPTER FIVE

Toni went over for supper around seven to find Rafe already waiting for her. There was something different about him, she decided during the meal, but nothing she could pin down exactly. A couple of times she caught him looking at her in a curious speculative fashion, and came to the conclusion that it wasn't really her he was seeing but rather a problem in his mind's eye. She would have liked to ask him if she could help in any way, but the chance seemed doubtful. Whatever it was, he would sort it out.

Later, in the privacy of Sean's little sitting room, there was an urgency to his lovemaking that had not been there before, at least not to the same degree. Responding to him blindly, Toni knew that the decision lay in her own hands. If she loved this man she should be ready to give him what he sought, regardless of what came after. Love didn't thrive on conditional surrender; she had found that out to her cost. If she had ever really loved Randy in the first place. Infatuation came very close, by all accounts. Close enough to mistake for the real thing. So was what she felt now for Rafe the real thing? She believed it was. She wanted desperately to believe it was. And yet . . .

As if sensing the struggle going on inside her, Rafe drew back, holding her lightly as he looked down into her face. His tone was understanding.

'Hardly creates the right atmosphere, does it? Maybe we should have installed soundproofing too.'

Until that moment Toni had been only vaguely aware of the disco music in the background, although now it was brought to her notice it did create a somewhat discordant note. It hadn't been bothering Rafe either until now, she realised, and knew this was his way of giving her time. The very fact that he was willing to keep a rein on his own obvious inclinations for her sake warmed her heart anew. So many men in these same circumstances would have carried right on regardless of any hesitation on her part—and probably succeeded too. He must be aware of that.

'Let's go for that swim,' he said softly. 'At least it will be quiet out by the lake. I'll go find a pair of trunks and meet you in front of the cabin. Ten minutes?'

She nodded, well aware that the moment would come again, if not tonight then certainly the next time he made love to her. But those times were limited, weren't they? Tomorrow night Sean would be back and her reason for staying on at Copper Lake would be gone. So would Rafe's, if it came to that. Would he remember his promise to take her around Calgary, or had that just been one of those things said on the spur of the moment?

The thought of not seeing him again was like an iron band about her chest. If only she could be sure of his feelings, sure that he wasn't simply playing with hers. Yet would he have spent so much time on her had his inten-tions not been more serious than a mere conquest? Rafe was a busy man; Sean had made that fact very clear. He was hardly going to take a week out just to seek the kind of fleeting gratification he could find almost anywhere with any woman, was he?

With the moon not yet risen it was dark enough outside the cabin for the eyes to take a moment or two to adjust properly. It took Rafe's movement away from the tree where he had been leaning to draw her attention. He was wearing a dark brown towelling robe of Sean's, which ended above his knees, the skin of his legs only a few shades lighter in colour beneath the coating of hair. The glance he ran over her own slender bikini-clad figure contracted her stomach muscles. She had never been as grateful as she was at this moment for the genes which made her the shape she was.

Rafe went into the water first, his body lithe and muscular above the dark trunks, turning beyond the line of reeds to tread water and thrust his hair out of his eyes.

'Come on,' he called softly. 'Not frightened of the dark, are you?'

Not the dark, Toni conceded, moving after him, but perhaps just a little of what he was doing to her. Where Rafe was concerned, she had no will of her own any more. She just wanted to be with him—any way he chose.

They swam together out towards the centre of the lake, keeping pace with a slow steady side-stroke which covered distance without overtaxing the strength. Toni was the first to take a rest, turning on her back to float under the stars while Rafe trod water close by.

'I'm not up to your standards,' she said, gently moving her hands to keep herself level. 'You could be across the lake while I'm still getting my first wind. Why don't you carry on for a while? I can make my own way back.'

'It isn't a marathon,' he came back, watching her. 'If a swim was all I wanted, I'd have come alone.'

Toni wouldn't look at him, her face upturned to the sky, body tingling with a sensation not wholly due to the movement of the water. 'What *do* you want, Rafe?' she whispered.

He came to her then, bringing her upright to face him and holding them both there by the movements of his legs. His face was tautly etched, water beaded on his skin. Toni put her hands against his chest as he caught her around the hips, spreading her fingers through the thick dark hair in a gesture that was more a plea than a protest.

'We'll sink!'

'So take a deep breath,' he said, and put his lips to hers as she instinctively obeyed, his legs coming about her to pin her calves together in a grip from which she could not escape.

The lake was deep at this point: deep enough to take them what seemed to be a long, long way down without touching bottom. Held close in Rafe's arms, Toni was aware of nothing but sensation: the softness of the water, the hardness of his body, the drumming, pounding beat of her heart in her ears. Then they were rising, breaking surface, and she was clinging to him, gasping for breath, the tumult inside her gathering momentum as he turned her on her back and began to tow her shorewards.

Grass grew thickly between the trees lining the lake edge. When Rafe laid her on it she made no protest, looking up into the strong dark features with eyes blurred by desire. His mouth on hers was fierce, demanding, not asking, rousing her beyond the point of coherent thought to a plane where fulfilment became the only need, the only wish, the only reason for existence.

Toni felt the touch of his fingers at her back, unfastening the clip of her top and easing it away from her body, the relative coolness of the night air on her skin. His hands and mouth were gentler now, exploring the firm softness of her breasts with a sensuality that drove her wild, moving down over her midriff to the flat plane of her stomach.

For a moment she couldn't understand the sudden sharp lift of his head. Then she heard the laughter, the sound of voices coming along the path from the direction of the lodge. Some people out for a late stroll, perhaps. Whatever the reason, they were coming this way.

They would be seen, Toni realised in swift darting panic. They couldn't fail to be seen! She pressed against Rafe's chest with both hands, body stiffened in rejection. 'Let me go!'

He did so without argument, rolling away to reach for his robe and hold it out to her.

'Put this on.'

Fingers nerveless, she huddled into the garment some-how, pulling the belt so tight about her middle she almost cut herself in two. The party was close enough now to be distinguishable as two couples, the women walking a pace or two ahead of their menfolk but obviously sharing the same conversation.

'Hi there,' said one of the former, seeing the two figures sitting under the trees. 'Been for a swim, have you? Good idea! We ought to have thought of that, Wal.' For the first time she seemed to realise the identity of the man with Toni, and her interest quickened. 'Should be getting on, I guess. How far round the lake does this trail go?'

It was Rafe who answered, his voice smooth and easy. 'About another half mile or so, then it turns off up into the trees. You'll have to come on back this way.'

'Oh, right, thanks.' She waved on the rest of the party with an exaggerated gesture. 'Come on, you guys!'

Toni found an answer for the chorus of goodnights as the quartet went on its way. She couldn't bear to look at Rafe. Another few moments and they would have been caught in the act with very little chance of concealing the fact. Every last element of desire had gone from her right now. She felt stripped naked in more ways than one.

'My fault,' Rafe acknowledged ruefully. 'I wasn't thinking straight.' He paused, viewing her unresponsive face, and a sound like a faint sigh escaped his lips. 'Toni——'

'I'm cold,' she said, not without truth. 'I think I'll go in.' She was glad of the darkness as she picked up the bikini top. 'I'll throw you out your robe if you'll just wait a minute.'

He came to his feet along with her, but made no attempt to touch her. 'We'll talk tomorrow,' he said. 'There's a lot needs saying. Just toss the robe over the rail. I'm going to take another dip.'

She heard the splash as she walked away towards the cottage, but she didn't turn round. There had been some different quality in his voice just now—a kind of wry regret. Yet he had little cause to feel guilty. She had wanted him as much as he had wanted her, and been just as unmindful of their surroundings.

She still wanted him, she acknowledged, only not the way it had so nearly happened tonight. She must make that clear to him tomorrow, even if it meant admitting to her own emotional involvement. If she loved him she owed him honesty.

It was a good fifteen minutes before she heard him come on to the step to fetch the robe she had draped over the rail as he had said. There was a pause during which she steeled herself for a tap on the door, but it didn't come. The creak of wood signalled Rafe's descent of the step again. She barely knew whether to be glad or sorry that he had made no further attempt to see her again tonight.

She was in bed, though far from sleep, when the knock did come on the door some half an hour later. Putting down the book in which she had been vainly attempting to lose herself, Toni lay gazing at the wood indecisively, wondering whether pretending to be asleep would do any good. Why Rafe had chosen to come back she wasn't at all certain. The only thing she did know was that she was neither mentally nor emotionally prepared for anything he had to say just yet.

The knock came again, this time accompanied by an appeal which brought her swiftly upright. 'Toni! It's Sean. I have to see you right away.'

She dragged on a wrap before going to open the door, looking at the familiar face in questioning surprise. 'I thought you weren't due back till tomorrow.'

'I wasn't, until I found out what I did find out this morning.' He looked beyond her to the empty room, taking in the recently vacated bed before coming back to her face to add hesitantly, 'Do you mind if I ask you a rather personal question?'

'At this time of night?' She tried to make light of it, sensing something coming that she wasn't going to like. 'Can't it wait till morning?'

'No.' The hesitancy vanished, and determination took its place. 'I have to know now. It's important.'

'To you or to me?' she queried.

'To us both.' He paused before saying it. 'Has Rafe tried anything with you?'

Her face went stiff. 'What's that supposed to mean exactly?'

'What it says. Has he been giving you the rush treatment?' He caught the sudden shift of expression in her eyes and his own went blank. 'The answer's yes, isn't it? He got to you.'

'No, he didn't get to me. Not the way you mean.' Toni deliberately closed her mind to the lack of total truth in that statement, knowing this went beyond mere sibling rivalry. 'Sean, what are you trying to say?'

He stood looking at her in silence for a long moment, the bleakness still there. 'Can I come inside?' he asked at last. 'It isn't easy to tell.'

Toni hesitated only a moment before drawing back to allow him entry. Whatever it was he had to say it wasn't going to be pleasant, that much was obvious. She felt the need to be within reach of a place to sit should the telling prove as painful as she was beginning to suspect.

With the door closed, Sean seemed uncertain of how to start. He refused a seat, standing with his hands on the back of a chair as if for support.

'How do you feel about him?' he asked at last. 'Rafe, I mean. How has he made you feel about him?'

She said thickly, 'I don't think that matters. Just tell me what you know that I don't.'

He sighed a little and spread his hands in a fleeting

gesture of contrition. 'I'm entirely to blame. I gave them the cause.'

'Them?'

'Rafe and my mother. They planned it between them. He was to come down here and get you into bed with him, just to prove to me how worthless you were.'

'Why?' Her voice was a whisper, her throat hurting so badly she could barely get the words out at all. 'Why should they have thought it necessary to prove anything to you about me?'

His face coloured uncomfortably. It took him a moment or two to force himself to say it. 'I told my mother I was in love with you and planned to ask you to marry me. That's why she sent for me to come home, and that's why Rafe came here. No way were they going to stand by and let me run my own life.'

'But why?' Toni asked again, dazed and un-comprehending. 'It wasn't true!'

'Who says it wasn't true?' For a moment there was belligerence in his voice, quickly subsiding before the expression on her face. His shrug was defensive. 'Okay, so maybe I laid it on a bit thick, but it wasn't so far from the truth. The way things were going it could easily have happened.'

'Could it?' She tried vainly to recall any moment in their relationship that might have led him to such a con-clusion, but could find none. 'Sean, I never gave you any reason to think about me that way. We were friends, that's all. Be honest about it. You never planned on asking me to marry you. I doubt if you've thought of marriage in any serious sense at all yet.'

He said slowly, 'You might be right—although if I did you'd be the kind of girl I'd want to marry.'

'Thanks.' She did her best not to let what she was feel-ing inside show through. 'All you have to do now is tell your brother you've seen the light, and he can go home happy.'

'It's not as simple as that.' He sounded anything but the latter emotion. 'You see, I kind of lost my head this morning when my mother let out what she and Rafe were up to. I told her no matter what happened I was still going to marry you, and I was coming right back here to ask you. If I know her, she'd be on the phone to warn Rafe the minute I left.'

'She didn't reach him till six,' Toni said dully. 'We were in Kamloops all day. It seems you've only two choices. You can admit the truth, or tell them I turned you down. Either way you're going to lose face.'

There was a pause before Sean spoke. When he did it was on a different note. 'Supposing we both of us save face? Think what a kick in the teeth it would be for Rafe if you told him you'd just been playing him along until I got back.' He shook his head at the look on her face. 'Not for real, but we'd be the only ones who'd know that. Come the right time, we'd just tell them we'd changed our minds.'

'It's ridiculous!' Her tone was sharp. 'What earthly good could it do?'

'For me, a whole lot. Prove I've got a mind of my own, for one thing. For you——' Sean paused, eyeing her speculatively—'wouldn't you like to pay him out in his own coin? Appear to, at any rate. Knowing Rafe the way I do, that would hit him right where it hurts. I doubt if he's ever had a woman lead *him* up a tree.'

Toni was silent, gazing at him with darkened eyes, conscious of the temptation rising so fiercely in her. Rafe had known no scruples, so why should she? He deserved some kind of put-down, and she could think of no better way. Recalling the feel of his hands on her body so little time ago, she knew a flash of sheer hatred. He would have taken her without compunction had they not been interrupted, reduced her to something lower than a common prostitute because he would at least have been paying for that service.

So let him pay another way, she decided. Let him know what it was like to have someone make a fool of him, even if it wasn't really true.

'All right,' she said, 'I'll do it.'

'Good! That'll show him. That'll show them both!' Sean paused a moment. 'Who's going to tell him?'

'Whoever sees him first.' Toni wanted suddenly and desperately to be alone. 'I hope it chokes him!'

'It will,' Sean assured her. 'Right up to the top.' He hesitated a moment longer, trying to find the right words. 'Toni, I'm sorry about all this. If it hadn't been for what I said, Rafe would never have acted the way he has. I should have suspected something similar when he said he was going to stay down here while I was in town, but——'

'But who'd have thought anyone would go to that amount of trouble to prove a simple point?' she finished for him. She had a grip on herself now; one she was going to keep. 'Don't worry about it, Sean. No damage done, beyond a dint in my pride.'

'Not as big as the one he's going to have, I'll bet. I'm not usually vindictive, but this time he's gone too far. They both have. They have to let me make my own mistakes; it's the only way I'm going to benefit from them.' He caught Toni's eyes and coloured a little. 'I didn't mean that the way it sounded.'

'I know how you meant it.' She felt as weary as she sounded. 'You'd better go now, Sean. It's late, and we're both going to need our sleep.'

'We've no plan of campaign,' he said. 'Look, we'll tell Rafe I came straight out here the moment I arrived and you said yes to me right away. And to make it even more authentic——' he was feeling in his pocket as he spoke, taking out a small square box—'you'd better wear this. Providing it fits.'

Toni gazed at the square-cut emerald and diamond ring revealed as he flipped up the lid without making any move to touch it. It wasn't new—the setting was too old-fashioned for that—but it was so obviously a valuable piece.

'Where did you get it?' she heard herself asking.

'It was left me by my grandmother to give to the girl I eventually married. I guess it never occurred to her that it wouldn't be every girl's choice. I collected it from the bank on my way here.'

'You were so sure I'd agree to go along?'

Something flickered in the hazel eyes. 'No, but I thought it best to come prepared.' The pause was brief, with an edge of concern. 'You're not changing your mind, are you?'

Toni thought of the last few days, and hardened her heart. 'No, I shan't change my mind. But I can't wear that ring, Sean. I might lose it.'

'It's insured. Anyway, you don't have to wear it all the time. Just enough to let Rafe see it. He knows what it was intended for.'

And it should have been saved for that purpose, Toni thought, but refrained from saying so. If it was what Sean wanted then she would go along. Anything in order to see the look on Rafe's face when he knew. She put out a surprisingly steady hand and took the ring from its bed, sliding it on to the third finger of her left hand with only a little difficulty.

'It's rather tight but not uncomfortable,' she said. 'You'd better leave me the box too, then I can put it away after it's served its purpose.'

Sean handed it over, his fingers touching hers in a gesture of encouragement. 'I'll see you in the morning, after I've seen Rafe. I'm looking forward to telling him. It will be the first time I ever got one up on him.'

Alone at last, Toni steeled herself against any desire to

indulge in self-pity. To a certain extent, she had asked for all she had got by being so gullible in the first place. Rafe's about-turn had been so sudden, so unfounded. She should have suspected some ulterior motive.

Not that her stupidity let him off the hook by any means. Revenge was going to be bitter-sweet. She refused to think beyond that point, sensing too many difficulties ahead. The here and now was all she cared about.

She slept little, awakening from a final, fitful doze around six-thirty. After last night the thought of bathing in the lake was anathema to her. She had to force herself to don a suit and go out into the still morning air, to run down the same bank where she had lain with Rafe and dive into the water, driving out the memories in swift, hard action.

He was waiting on the step when she got back to the cottage. Eyes on the ground, Toni failed to see him until she was almost on him. She felt her whole body tense as she looked up to meet the steely grey gaze.

'I just got through talking to Sean,' he said. 'Now let me hear it from you.'

If there had been any wavering in her resolve at all his tone was all the spur she needed. She stood her ground, looking at him squarely, towel slung about her shoulders. 'Sean asked me to marry him and I said yes. Does that cover it?'

'Why Sean?' His voice was still controlled. 'He won't be worth anything for another two years.'

'That's a matter of opinion.' She forced herself to ignore the implication. 'Personally, I think he's worth ten of you right now!'

He said it very softly. 'You didn't seem to think that way so much last night.'

Toni could feel the warmth rising in her face despite all her efforts to stop it. It took everything she had to lift her shoulders in wry acknowledgement.

'I'm afraid I got a little carried away last night. You are rather persuasive, Rafe. But then that was the idea, wasn't it? A pity those people had to come by at the wrong moment and ruin a whole week's work. Not that it would have made any difference to the way Sean feels about me. He's already told his mother that much.'

It seemed an age before Rafe moved or spoke. A blank mask seemed to be drawn over his face, robbing it of all expression save for the pulsing of a solitary nerve near the corner of his mouth.

'You're trying to tell me you were playing me along the whole time?' he asked at last, and she shivered inwardly at the tone of his voice.

'There's no law against two playing the same game, is there? As a matter of fact, I quite enjoyed it. You must have made love to a lot of women in your time to have gained so much experience!'

The mockery was registering with him; she could see that in his eyes. But there was no change of expression in his face to signal his intention as he moved with all the speed of a striking cobra to take hold of her. Thrust ahead of him into the cottage, Toni made no effort to resist, aware of his superior strength and all too mindful of the last time. She turned on him as he kicked the door shut behind him, feeling the towel slip to the floor.

'Come near me and you'll have Sean to answer to! Or don't you care?'

'About Sean? Yes, I care.' The lean features were grim. 'Which is why I'm not going to stand by and see him make a mess like this of his life. You win. Name your price.'

Her lip curled. 'Everything comes down to money with you. I don't have a price.'

'You're not trying to tell me you're in love with him?'

'I'm not trying to tell you *any*thing,' she flung back. 'I doubt if you'd listen. Just get out of here!'

He had her by the shoulders, drawing her up to him, his fingers digging into her flesh. 'I said are you in love with him?'

'No.' Even now she could not bring herself to depart wholly from the truth. 'But I wouldn't find it hard to be. He's the only one of you I've ever met who was worth loving!'

There was no slackening of his grip. His mouth looked cruel: a thin hard line. 'You've got him hog-tied, haven't you? In two years you'll have him ready to jump through hoops if you say so. Well, I'm not going to let that happen, do you hear? I'll show you for what you are!'

Toni stared unwaveringly into the grey eyes, hating him for the power his very touch still had to stir her senses. 'Good luck! You'll need it. Sean's finished with letting you and his mother run his life for him!'

His mouth came down hard on hers, the thrust of his tongue between her clenched lips its own searing comment. Then he was stepping back from her, contempt in his glance.

'I was right about you the first time. You're out for what you can get. Just don't be too surprised if what you do get turns out to be rather different from what you expect.'

It was deathly quiet for several minutes after he had left. The sound of a motor being started up along the lake was a welcome intrusion on her thoughts. Toni stirred herself numbly, aware that Sean might be along any moment.

The first thing she was going to have to tell him was that she couldn't go through with this deception. The taste of revenge was sour, not sweet. She wanted no more of it. If she moved fast, she could be away from here in half an hour. Once she reached Calgary, she would book herself a seat on the first available flight home to England. The fact that she would be arriving there practically destitute was one she refused to think about right now. One step at a time was how she had to take it.

She was almost packed by the time Sean did arrive. He stood in the open doorway looking at her in stunned silence for several seconds before he spoke.

'Toni, you can't change your mind now,' he burst out at last on a note of concern. 'I thought you wanted to put one across on Rafe as much as I did?'

She folded a shirt with meticulous care, not meeting his eyes. 'I thought so too. Somehow it doesn't seem important any more.' She blinked hard to clear her vision, determined to show no emotion. 'I'm sorry, Sean, but that's it. I'm leaving. Your ring is in its box on the table over there.'

'You gave me your word.' His voice was quiet but determined. 'If you break it you're not the person I thought you were.'

She turned on him then, eyes sparkling. 'I'm not the person *I* thought I was, so what difference does it make? You have to sort out your own problems, Sean, I can't help you.'

'I can't, and you can.' He came across to take her by the arms, drawing her round to face him. There was appeal in his eyes. 'Please, Toni, don't run out on me. Not now when I've just made my first stand. It will all have been for nothing if you go.'

'You can do it without me,' she said in desperation. 'You don't need anyone else to back you up. You're a person in your own right, Sean, not just an extension of the Stewart clan!'

'But you're the only one who can keep me convinced of that. That's why I need you—to give me confidence in myself.' He paused, searching her face with entreaty. 'Just for a short time, that's all I'm asking. You don't care about Rafe. It's only your pride that's hurt.' This time the pause was questioning. 'Isn't it?'

It was pride that refused to allow her to admit the truth. The word came out without prompting. 'Yes.'

'Then what's wrong with taking a dig at him? If you leave now he'll have won. He'll think it's because you're afraid of him.'

Toni was afraid, but not in a sense she could make Sean understand without giving herself away. She spread her hands helplessly. 'I don't have a job any longer, and I have to turn in my car some time.'

'That's okay. We'll both drive back to Calgary.' There was a new decisiveness in his voice. 'I've finished with this place. Rafe can put in a manager. You'll stay at the house, of course.'

'No!' The refusal was jerked from her. 'I couldn't do that.'

'As my fiancée and with nowhere else to go, you'd be expected to.' Sean added urgently, 'Toni, you were the one who told me to stand up to my family. Do you want to be the one responsible for putting me back lower than where I started?'

Her shoulders slumped suddenly and defeatedly. 'You know,' she said on a flat note of acceptance, 'in some ways you're just as ruthless as your brother.'

'I'm learning,' Sean returned. 'I'm learning all the time. Does that mean it's on again?'

'I suppose so.' She made a weak attempt to regain some initiative. 'But only for a limited period.'

He was smiling now. 'Thanks. You don't know what this means to me.'

She had a better idea of what it was going to mean to her, and the knowledge was not encouraging. Committing herself to a scheme like this had been crazy in the first place, but committed she was.

'Come on over for breakfast,' Sean invited. 'Things always seem better on a full stomach.'

Toni wasn't sure about that, but she went with him

anyway. She had to face Rafe again some time, and probably the sooner the better in this case.

The latter was drinking coffee in the dining room. He watched the two of them coming without change of expression.

'We didn't eat yet,' announced Sean somewhat unnecessarily. 'Mind if we join you?'

'I'm almost through,' came the brief rejoinder, 'but feel free.'

Toni sat down opposite, forcing herself to meet the grey eyes. The coldness she saw there made her shiver. It was difficult right now to believe that only a few short hours ago she had lain in this man's arms, had felt that hard mouth of his so soft and tender on her skin, his hands so warmly possessive. All pretence on his part, of course. That was what hurt so much. All? Her own mouth took on a cynical line. Not quite. His physical reactions had been real enough.

'What are your plans?' asked the subject of her thoughts, lifting a sardonic eyebrow in response to his brother's swift glance. 'You must have made plans.'

'Some,' Sean admitted with seeming reluctance, then rallied to add on a firmer note, 'I'm taking Toni home to meet Mother. Anybody could run this place now. I've had enough.'

A shrug was the only comment. 'How are you getting there?'

'By road, obviously. Toni has to turn in her car. I'll follow on behind.'

'When?'

Sean looked momentarily disconcerted, not having got quite that far. 'Tomorrow maybe. There's no tearing rush.'

'I'm almost packed,' put in Toni, suddenly anxious to be clear of this place and all its associations. 'We could leave today.' She looked back levelly at the older man.

'Just think, if you'd let me go when Bill came back I might have been home in England right now!'

'I'd have followed you,' declared Sean with convincing certainty. His laugh held a hint of malice. 'Lacking in tenacity, didn't you say not so long ago, Rafe? Well, not this time. This time nothing is going to put me off!'

Come the time when this mock engagement ended, Rafe was going to remember that statement, thought Toni, watching the grey eyes. Remember it and use it. Sean should have more sense than to keep on underlining the non-existent permanency of this arrangement of theirs. At the best she might stick it out a month—and even that was going to take some doing.

'I'll let Karen know you're on your way,' said Rafe, making the decision for them. 'She'll want to make sure a room is ready.'

Sean hesitated for a moment, then let it pass. 'I guess there's no real cause to wait till tomorrow. Who will you bring in to take my place?'

'I don't think that need concern you too much,' came the short response. He got to his feet, face set in grim, unrelenting lines as his eyes found Toni's. 'I'll be seeing you.'

She recognised the threat without reacting to it. In no way was Rafe Stewart going to be content to sit back and accept the situation as it appeared to him. Yet what could he do? Certainly nothing he told Sean was going to make any difference. He was stuck with it until the moment when she and his brother decided to end the charade.

There was no sign of him when they left around ten. Driving away from the lake which had been her home for the last few weeks, Toni was conscious of a sense of loss. She had been happy there before Rafe had come to disrupt her equanimity, happier in many ways than she had been in years. Had it not been for him she could have looked back on the whole episode with pleasant nostalgia. She felt robbed.

With Sean sitting somewhat too closely on her tail, the drive up through Kicking Horse Valley was accomplished in rather less time than Toni would have cared for had she been alone. The scenery was magnificent, the road crossing and recrossing the river via a series of twists and bends which brought ever more spectacular views of the glacial mountains. At this time of year the river itself had narrowed to a fraction of its springtime torrent, but the wide flood plains isolating the tiny community of Field were ample indication of the kind of devastation the melting snows could bring.

Apart from the broad, well-metalled highway and the occasional settlement, the landscape out here could have changed little in thousands of years, Toni reflected. It was still pioneer country, wild and beautiful and unlikely ever to be tamed. Some day she would like to come back and see other parts of it. Some day . . .

Inevitably she found her thoughts turning to the ordeal that lay ahead. Meeting Karen Stewart for the first time was not going to be easy, especially knowing as she did that her very presence in the Stewart household was unjustified. What she and Sean were doing was deceitful and dishonest, no matter what the provocation on either side. And what good would it do in the end? Sean was going to find himself right back where he had started once he proved himself apparently incapable of fulfilling yet another role.

The B.C.–Alberta border lay over a mile above sea level, according to the guide book Toni was carrying. On impulse, she signalled to the vehicle behind and turned into the first convenient layby, switching off the engine and easing herself out from behind the wheel to stretch her limbs in some relief.

Shining from a sky devoid of any masking haze, the sun had a power totally at odds with the surrounding white-

capped peaks. Admiring the view, she felt at odds herself—torn between conflicting emotions. Helping Sean
was one thing, but where was it going to leave her?

'Tired?' he asked, coming up behind her at the low
wall edging the steep drop to the valley below. 'I thought
we were going to keep going till we hit Banff?'

'I need to talk,' she said. '*We* need to talk, Sean.' She
turned her head a little to look at him, aware of a tight-
ening of the muscles around her heart as her eyes rested
on certain familiarities. The father showed so clearly in
both brothers; to look at one was to see the other. Just
now she didn't want to think about Rafe.

'Supposing you told your mother the truth about us,'
she said. 'It might make her realise just what she and
Rafe are doing to you.'

The shake of his head was emphatic. 'It wouldn't work.
You'll see that for yourself once you meet her.'

'I'm not sure I want to meet her. Not this way. I feel a
total fraud!'

It was a moment or two before he answered, his face
tense as he studied her. 'I hate doing this,' he said in the
end, 'but can you afford a ticket home if I refuse to pay
the rental on your car?'

She gazed at him in defeat, recognising the determination in him. 'You should leave that kind of pressure to
your brother,' she said on a bitter note. 'He doesn't have
a conscience to trouble him.'

'I'm sorry.' The apology was sincere. 'I just can't let
you run out on me now. It's too—important.'

'To you. What about me?'

His smile lacked buoyancy. 'You don't have to tell me
I'm being selfish. I know. But I'll make it up to you,
Toni. Just give me the chance.'

'I don't seem to have much choice.' She came away
from the wall. 'All right, I let myself in for this, so I
deserve to pay for it. How much farther to Banff?'

'About forty miles. If we take an hour for lunch we should make Calgary by four at the latest. We'll turn in your car first, then go out to the house in mine. Okay?'

'It has to be, doesn't it?'

'Don't be like that,' he pleaded. 'I need you.'

'Not as much as you think.' Toni gave him a reluctant smile, knowing herself trapped. 'You'd better take the lead from here. I'll just follow on.'

CHAPTER SIX

BANFF was a fairytale town in a fairytale setting, so crowded with tourists it took them almost an hour to find a place to eat.

'Should have known better,' Sean admitted over coffee. 'This time of year the Parks are always crowded. Lots of folks only get as far as this and think they've seen all that's worth seeing, yet it's only a few miles to the Icefields Parkway over to Jasper. You should see the glaciers up there—they're unbelievable! You can even ride across Athabasca in a snowmobile.'

'I'll have to take your word for it,' said Toni, smiling a little at his enthusiasm. 'You don't have to sell me on this country of yours, Sean. I'm more than willing to go along with any superlative you can apply.'

'Think you could live here?' he asked on a casual note. 'In preference to England, I mean.'

'In preference, no. I don't think there's ever anything quite like one's own country. If circumstances warranted it——' she paused, trying not to think about the only circumstances which might—'well, it wouldn't be any hardship. Shouldn't we be going? The car hire office might close early on a Friday.'

'No problem. We could always take it in tomorrow if necessary.'

'All the same——'

'Okay.' He lifted a hand to beckon the waitress. 'Whatever you say.'

The mountains were left behind now, dwindling to a jagged line on the horizon as the city came into view at last. A modern city, skyscrapers tall in the centre and still growing; spreading out to fill the plain. Toni viewed it with detachment. She was here purely as a transient, soon to be gone again—though not soon enough.

Sean insisted on paying the rental charges after all, reading her correctly in his assumption that the gesture put her under more of an obligation to him than if he had failed to trust her. With her luggage transferred into his own car, they were on their way again inside fifteen minutes. Toni was quiet as they moved through the busy city streets, dreading the approaching confrontation. She was only thankful that Rafe wasn't going to be present, although she had to face him again some time, of course.

'We're quite some way out of town,' Sean advised, sensing her preoccupation. 'My father had the house built new when he married again. Rafe keeps a couple of horses so you'll be able to ride when you feel like it.'

Her laugh was short. 'I doubt if he'll be feeling generous enough to offer me the use. You seem to be forgetting what happened.'

There was a small silence before he answered. 'I never found out what did happen—not exactly. I know he made love to you, but——'

'But you're not sure just how far it went.' Her throat felt tight. 'Why not ask your brother?'

'I wouldn't give him the satisfaction. Anyway, it doesn't matter. He lost.'

On the surface, she thought painfully. Only on the surface.

The Stewart estate was even larger than she had anticipated. From the wide white gateway to the house itself they clocked up almost half a kilometre. Two-storeyed, and imposingly fronted, the house offered her little welcome. It looked what it was: the home of a rich and powerful family. She could only be glad that her residence was not to be permanent.

Inside the house was no less impressive. The entrance

lobby alone had to be twenty feet square, the double-width staircase rising from it to meet an open gallery. Sean instructed a manservant to bring in his own and Toni's luggage from the car, then led the way across to one of the big mahogany doors, taking her arm reassuringly as they reached it.

'For better or for worse,' he said, 'this is it. Don't let me down.'

There was no time to reply because he was opening the door, ushering her forward into a room full of light from the west-facing windows. A beautiful room furnished with taste and discretion, the long silk curtains a perfect complement to the thick gold-coloured carpet and warm, glowing wood. From here the mountains looked almost close enough to reach out and touch, their rugged slopes softened by the early evening sun.

The woman seated in the wheelchair facing the view made no immediate effort to turn on their entry. Cut short to follow the lines of her well-shaped head, her smooth dark hair showed no trace of grey.

'I expected you earlier,' she said without particular inflection. 'Rafe said you left at ten.'

She came round to face them then, controlling the chair electrically via a series of buttons set into an arm. At forty-four, Karen Stewart was still a very beautiful woman, her features fine and regular. Her eyes were so dark a brown they were almost black, their impact hypnotic. A long red skirt hid the useless legs.

'So you're my son's choice,' she said, returning Toni's scrutiny. Her smile was unexpected. 'It's going to be nice having another woman to talk to. Would you like tea? I ordered some to be brought in the minute you arrived.'

'Thank you, I'd love it.' Toni felt totally at a loss. Whatever she had anticipated it had not been this. She glanced at Sean, seeing the same confusion she felt mirrored in his eyes.

'You were expecting opposition both of you, weren't you?' Karen sounded amused. 'You came in here ready to fight.'

It was Sean who answered. 'Yesterday you said I'd marry Toni over your dead body.'

The smile didn't falter. 'Yesterday we both said a whole lot of things best forgotten. I've had time to think since then, to realise that you're of an age to make your own decisions, right or wrong.'

'This one isn't wrong!'

'Did I say it was?' Her tone was gentle. 'Only the two of you can decide that question. All I ask is that you give yourselves the time to be sure.' She patted the arm of the sofa against which she had stopped her chair. 'Come and sit down, Toni, and tell me a little about yourself.'

'Hasn't Rafe already done that?' she asked with deliberation.

'Only so far as he knows it—or thinks he knows it. Knowing Craig Shannon the way I do, I think you deserve at least the benefit of the doubt.' She broke off at a sound from outside. 'Here comes the tea, specially in your honour. Sean, you might open the door for Luis—save him putting down the tray. Do come and sit down, Toni.'

Toni went, albeit with reluctance. The whole situation felt wrong. Here was a woman doing her utmost to overcome implanted prejudice, and she wasn't even entitled to be here at all. Sean had given her the wrong impression of his mother. Her interference could have stemmed only from concern for his welfare, and who could blame her for that? Mothers were always reluctant to give up their sons, she had heard; more especially so perhaps in the case of a widow with no man of her own to fall back on. Sean must be made to realise how unfair this deception of theirs was.

Sean brought the tray across himself, setting it down on

the sofa table in front of Toni. There was a silent plea in
the eyes meeting hers as he straightened. Don't give the
game away, it said.

It was difficult to avoid doing so during the following
moments of wholly amicable conversation. Far from
quizzing Toni's background, Karen seemed interested
only in her impressions of Canada as a future home, in-
creasing the sense of guilt with every word. Toni scarcely
knew whether to be relieved or dismayed when Rafe
walked into the room.

Sean revealed himself under no such dilemma, jerking
upright in his seat as if propelled by a spring. 'When did
you decide to come home?' he demanded.

'About an hour after you left,' came the reply. 'Once
I'd settled the question of who I was going to bring in to
take over from you there seemed little point in staying on.
The new man will be there now. He was flying charter up
from Vancouver.' His gaze came to rest on Toni and took
on a harder light. 'Enjoy your trip?'

'Very much.' Her tone was subdued. She had needed
time to prepare herself for seeing Rafe again. Deprived of
it, she had no armour.

Rafe waited a moment as if expecting more, than
shrugged and went to pour himself a drink from the cabi-
net in the far corner, turning back to the room with glass
in hand and irony in his smile.

'Anyone feel like proposing a toast?'

'You're the only one drinking,' his brother pointed
out shortly. 'Propose your own.'

'Fair enough.' It was no accident that the grey eyes
had come to rest once more on green. 'To new relations!'

'I'm tired,' announced Karen suddenly into the small
silence which followed. She looked it too, her face drawn.
'I think I'll go and lie down before supper.'

Rafe put down the glass without having tasted the con-
tents. 'I'll see you up.'

The offer was accepted in the manner of one accustomed to such solicitude. To Toni she said briefly, 'You'll have to forgive me. We'll talk again later.'

Toni waited until the door was closed before voicing the question. 'Is she often in pain like that?'

'As often as she wants to be,' said her son without emotion. 'That's something you'll learn.'

'She can't have been pretending just then,' Toni protested, shocked by his attitude. 'You saw her face. She looked as pale as death!'

'I'm not saying she's pretending. Just that it seems to come on at the moments she chooses.'

'Psychosomatic, you mean?' Her brows creased a little. 'If that's true, why now?'

'Because of Rafe. To prove he's still hers even if I'm not.' He shrugged at the look on her face. 'You don't have to take my word for it. Just use your eyes. It happens often enough.'

It was a moment or two before she responded, her voice low. 'If you're right why doesn't he see it himself?'

'Maybe he does. Who knows? It wouldn't make any difference.'

'I don't understand.'

'It's simple enough.' Sean sounded as hard as his brother right then, his face set. 'Considering he's responsible for the way she is.'

The silence seemed to grow about them, broken only by an odd whining sound from somewhere in the house. Lift, an element of Toni's mind supplied without being asked. 'How?' she got out at last.

'He was driving the car they were all of them in at the time—nineteenth birthday present. Another car hit them when he was crossing an intersection. Dad was killed outright.'

And his mother crippled for life. Toni didn't say the words; they were burned into her brain. 'And Rafe?'

she heard herself ask.

'He walked away with hardly a scratch.'

She sat with closed eyes, imagining what the moment of realisation must have been like. At nineteen, what had Rafe himself been like?

'They said he wasn't at fault,' Sean went on in the same emotionless manner. 'The other car went through a stop sign. If he hadn't been driving too fast he'd have seen it coming.'

'You can't be sure he was driving too fast,' she protested softly. 'If the police said it wasn't his fault it hardly seems likely.'

'He always drove too fast. She used to encourage him.'

'Your mother?'

'Who else?' His voice had acquired a certain bitterness. 'With her it was always Rafe. I didn't have enough spirit for her.'

'What about your father?'

'From what I remember he was rather quiet, even reserved. Rafe supposedly takes after his mother so far as temperament goes. Attraction of opposites, isn't it called?'

Repeated in his second marriage, Toni reflected. Only this time the result of that union had taken after him. Had he been disappointed? Worse still, had he revealed that disappointment to his younger son? There was no reason to suppose so. It appeared to be only towards his mother that Sean felt any bitterness.

She was becoming involved, she realised with dismay. In spite of everything, she was allowing her emotions to take over. She had to make herself stand back from the situation – to view it with detachment. She was here to play a part, nothing more.

'I'd like to have a shower and change my clothes,' she said. 'Can you show me which room I'll be in?'

'I can always find it. I know the options.' Sean rose abruptly. 'Let's go and look.'

Rafe was not in evidence on the upper floor. Toni wondered if he could still be with Karen, and knew a swift, sharp pang before she took a hold on herself. That was not the nature of the relationship, nor ever could be. What existed between the two of them was far more complex. For fifteen years Rafe had lived with the constant reminder of terrible tragedy. How did that affect a man's mind? How could it not affect him?

Her room overlooked a paved area of garden containing a swimming pool, with the mountains off to the right. From the small balcony Toni could see outbuildings and a corral beyond a thin belt of trees. Perhaps she might wander over later on and take a closer look. Rafe could hardly object to that.

'I shouldn't have asked you to come here, should I?' said Sean unexpectedly from the doorway behind her. 'You were right, I was only thinking of myself.'

She turned to look at him, responding to the dejection in his voice with a wryly acknowledging smile. 'Perhaps not, but now that I am here we can't do much else but see it through. I thought your mother seemed pretty well adjusted to the idea considering the way it was sprung on her. The thing I don't like is lying to her.'

'Then don't,' he said with sudden urgency. 'It doesn't have to be a lie, Toni. We could make the engagement real.'

She stared at him without moving, realising he was serious. 'Sean——' she began slowly, 'I don't——'

'I know you don't love me,' he broke in, 'but you're as much in need of someone as I am of you. We could make a go of it. Just give it a chance!'

He had never seemed so young as he did at that moment. Toni barely knew what to say to him—how to make him understand.

'It isn't just a matter of not being in love with you,' she said at length. 'We just aren't—balanced. I need someone older, while you——'

'Like Rafe?' he demanded with bitter inflection. 'Everything was fine till he came along!'

'Not Rafe.' She made the denial with a fierceness of her own. 'There's no way I could marry a man like your brother!'

'You wouldn't get the chance. My mother would see to that—the way she saw to it the other times.'

'Other times?' The question was torn from her.

'Twice Rafe has brought a girl home to meet her. Both times she became so ill it was pitiful to see her. Finally he got the message, and since then he's kept whatever love life he has strictly to himself. She's never going to let him go, not while she's alive. Me, maybe, but not Rafe. He made her the way she is and he has to pay for it.'

'That's sick!'

'Who's arguing? It's the way things are.'

'But don't you see? By giving in to her Rafe is just making the situation worse. Sometimes it's necessary to be cruel to be kind.'

'That's his problem. I want out.' He paused, tone changing. 'Toni——'

'It's no use, Sean.' She said it as gently as she could. 'I don't feel that way about you. I think it would be better if I went.'

'No, please.' He sounded unhappy. 'I shan't make a nuisance of myself, I promise. If you leave now I'm going to look a complete idiot. Once it's accepted that I'm a free agent we'll stage a break-up. I'll even put you on a plane home myself.'

He who hesitates is lost, Toni thought, and knew it applied to herself in this case. She said wearily, 'All right. I don't like it, but I'll stay. What time is dinner? I still have to change.'

'We usually eat around seven when it's just family. That gives you almost an hour.' Sean waited a brief moment, then made a resigned little gesture. 'I'll see you then.'

Sean was not in love with her, she comforted herself when she was alone at last. He simply needed someone to support him in his fight for independence. Rafe was another matter. It didn't seem possible that he would allow himself to be manipulated in any way, much less this one. The accident had been a terrible stroke of fate for which he could not be blamed. What Karen was doing to him went beyond justice.

Showered, she felt better about things, if only slightly. There was something about running water which lifted the spirits despite oneself. Negative ions, wasn't it? Right now she could have used an overdose.

She put on a cool cotton print in pale green, eyeing her reflection in the long dressing mirror with a certain disfavour. It was the way she looked which brought all the problems. If she were a plain Jane she'd probably be a great deal happier.

And that was rubbish too, she acknowledged almost at once. Her gullibility was the real problem. To survive she had to start looking deeper beneath the surface—use a little more of that so-called feminine intuition. Starting with Karen Stewart, perhaps.

There was no opportunity to start that evening because Karen did not come down to dinner. She was taking the meal in her room, Rafe said. Alone with the two brothers, Toni found the atmosphere overwhelmingly brittle. She was not at all surprised when Rafe took his leave as soon as they finished eating.

'I'm not sure how long I'm going to be able to take this,' she confessed to Sean as the door closed behind the older man. 'It isn't even as if I had right on my side.'

'He doesn't have it on his either,' came the short response. He was tracing the weave of the fine white cloth with the tip of his coffee spoon, ignoring the faint brown stain he had left in his wake. When he looked up it was suddenly, as if he hoped to catch her out in some way. 'How do you really feel about him, Toni?'

She was silent for a while, not at all certain herself. 'I don't hate him,' she said at length. 'He couldn't have got anywhere without my co-operation. If he's as trapped as you say, I can even feel sympathy for him.'

'He wouldn't thank you for it.'

'He doesn't have to. I doubt if I'll be extending it.' She stirred restlessly, aware of the evening stretching ahead. 'Do you think he'd have any objection if I strolled across and had a look at his horses?'

'Can't see why he should if you're only looking.' Sean hesitated. 'You don't want me to come with you?'

She shook her head. 'I'd rather be alone for a while if you don't mind. Even if the engagement were real we wouldn't have to live in each other's pockets.'

'No, I guess not.' He sounded downcast. 'I said I wouldn't make a nuisance of myself, and I meant it, only it's going to look a bit odd if we don't spend any time at all together. The Stampede started today. I thought we might go down to the grounds tomorrow.'

'That sounds a good idea,' Toni said gently. 'I'll look forward to it, Sean. I think I'll turn in when I've had my walk. It's been a long day.'

He made no demur, seemingly prepared to go along with anything she suggested. There was little else he could do, she reflected dryly, considering that he was the one who needed help—or thought he did. All he really needed was a little more of the kind of determination he had shown in getting her here. Faced with that, both mother and brother might start taking him seriously.

The air was still and warm, the humidity down to a comfortable degree. Skirting the swimming pool, Toni took a path cutting across directly to the corral, strolling along with hands tucked into the pockets of her dress. Apart from one or two small flying bugs there seemed relatively little livestock about. The lack of mosquitoes was a relief in itself. There had been times out at the lake when they had driven her mad—one of the penalties of living close to open water.

Inevitably her thought turned to the previous night, and the pain stirred in her. The pre-design was what hurt so much: to know that every kiss, every caress had been carefully calculated towards the one ultimate end. If only it were possible to hurt him in the same way. It wasn't, of course. He was impregnable. That was something she was going to have to accept.

The two horses were both fine animals, as she had known they would be, one of them a big chestnut stallion with powerful quarters, the other a dark roan gelding friendly enough to approach the fence when Toni leaned on it.

'You're too trusting to belong to who you do belong to,' she told the animal softly as she stroked the head thrust inquisitively across her. 'You should be more like your stable-mate over there and stay aloof!'

'Too bad he's lacking in horse sense,' agreed Rafe dryly from almost right beside her. 'Bored with Sean's company already?'

She gave the animal a last rub before turning slowly, willing herself to stay cool and calm. 'Not at all,' she said. 'I felt like a walk and he didn't. Anyway, he doesn't have any interest in horses.'

'True.' He rested an elbow on the rail, lifting a foot to a lower one. He was wearing jeans, the material tight about lean hips. The eyes holding hers were sardonic. 'Now tell me the real reason you came over here.'

It was a moment before she took his meaning, her mouth compressing as she did so. 'I didn't know you were here. If I had it would have been the last place I'd have visited!'

'Sure.' He made no effort to conceal his disbelief. 'You

just wanted to see the horses.'

'That's right.' Toni said it firmly and clearly. 'And having done that I'm quite ready to go. Goodnight.'

He caught her before she had taken two paces, swinging her round to face him again. The glitter in his eyes held more than anger.

'You're not going to marry Sean,' he gritted. 'If it's the last thing I do, I'll stop that happening!'

His touch was like fire on her skin; she could feel herself trembling, the swift aching desire coursing through her. He was right, she was not going to marry Sean. But the choice was hers, not his, and one she would announce in her own time.

'How?' she asked. 'He's of age, and in full possession of all his faculties. There's nothing you can do to stop it.'

'There's this,' he said, and pulled her to him.

Held taut against the hard body she couldn't fight and didn't want to fight. All she wanted was for this moment to go on in perpetuity, shutting out the rest of the world. It couldn't be like that, of course. The world refused to be shut out. Memory lent her the strength of mind to stop the blind response.

'More instructions from your stepmother?' she said when he lifted his head. 'Too bad you can't live up to her expectations of you, Rafe.'

His voice was quiet but not soft. 'Leave Karen out of it. This is for me. I'm going to break you, Toni. I'll make you sorry you ever set eyes on Copper Lake!'

She was that already, but she refrained from saying so. There was no way she was going to let him intimidate her now. Let him do his worst. She faced up to him squarely. 'I don't break easily.'

'We'll see.' He let her go, standing back from her with a hard twist of his lips. 'We'll see just how tough you really are.'

Toni made herself walk away slowly, feeling anything

but tough. Staying on here was going to prove a feat of
endurance, but she would see it through. Only when Rafe
finally accepted that he was not going to drive her out
would she be ready to leave, and on that day she would
have the pleasure of telling him the truth. It was a thought
to keep her going.

It was almost dark by the time she reached her room—
too dark to see more than the blur of trees fronting the
corral. Yet somehow she knew Rafe would still be there,
watching for her light. She put one on before drawing the
curtains, standing for a moment in the balcony doorway
looking across. Let him see her doing it! Let him take it
the way it was meant—as a challenge to him. She even
lifted a hand in mocking salute before closing out the
night.

Surprisingly she slept well, awakening to a morning
bright with sun. The Canadian summers might be short,
but while they lasted they were what summers should be.
Even in winter one knew just what to expect. It gave life
a certain regularity missing from the English scene.

Sean was alone in the dining room when she went
down. Rafe, he said, had already left the house on business
unspecified and his mother never came down to breakfast.

'If we're going to the Stampede grounds you're over-
dressed,' he commented, eyeing her linen slacks and shirt.
'Jeans and boots are the order of the day. Do you have
any boots?'

Toni shook her head, smiling at the thought. 'I planned
on waiting till the appropriate time to buy things like
that. Originally, that is. I doubt if I'll still be here come
the colder weather.'

'Just jeans, then—and maybe a checked shirt? We can
get you a hat when we get there.' He paused, watching
her, a question in his eyes. 'You never told me why you
came to Canada in the first place.'

She had no intention now either. She smiled again, and shrugged. 'I needed a change. With no other ties, it seemed worthwhile making it a big one. How long does the Stampede last?'

'Ten days.' If Sean recognised a deliberate change of subject he gave no sign. 'And it isn't confined to the showgrounds. The whole city gets in on the act. Tonight we'll go into town and look up one or two people—have ourselves a party, or maybe join up with someone else's. Anything goes Stampede week!'

Toni was silent for a moment, viewing the prospect without any great enthusiasm. A rave-up—and that was what it sounded like—was hardly her scene. 'Do I play your fiancée for them too?' she asked.

Now it was Sean's turn to be quiet, his eyes reflecting inner conflict. 'There's no point otherwise,' he said at length. 'We don't have to make a big thing out of it.'

We don't; others might, she thought, but there was resignation in it. She was up to her neck already; a little deeper wasn't going to make any difference.

Dominated by the red-masted heights of the Calgary Tower, the downtown area of the city looked from a distance as if it might have been set there en bloc by some gigantic hand, its edges sharply defined. They drove through the centre of it to reach the Exhibition ground, leaving the car parked on a back street while they joined the throngs of Western-garbed people all making their way to the same destination.

Old and young alike joined in the spirit of the occasion, sporting shirts bouncing with fringing, and stetson hats in every imaginable hue. There was a carnival feeling in the air.

The whole thing was bigger, more elaborate than Toni had visualised. Smiling to herself, she had to admit that in her mind's eye she had seen Calgary itself as little more than the cattle town it had once been. Walking through a

Midway not yet into its daily swing, one had to be aware of the vast amount of planning which must go into this yearly event. Worthwhile, of course, for the profits it must bring to the town, but a tremendous effort nevertheless.

Inside the huge grandstand building, she found herself in a world of bright modern decor and cool tiled floors, of smoothly running escalators and orderly traffic flow.

'We're infield,' Sean told her, leading the way up a ramp to emerge in the hot sunshine of the stadium. 'Over there behind the chutes.'

The infield seats were ranked in metal tiers built right over the animal pens themselves, with a canvas canopy to protect the watchers from the full heat of the day. To reach them they traversed a tunnel below the race track and climbed to the level of the uppermost tier by way of a boarded walk stretched between metal supports, dropping down again to find their own seats on the front row immediately over Number Six chute gate. The animal smell was strong and pungent in the air, emotive of a time when cattle and horses were all this region knew in the way of wealth. Oil, Toni thought, could never smell one half as sweet!

The chuckwagon racing which began the morning's entertainment was a revelation in itself. Competing for a sizeable chunk of the overall prize money, thirty-two wagons ran in eight heats of four to decide a winner who not only had to be possessed of courage and daring, but also, so far as Toni could see, a fair degree of death-wish into the bargain. Twice the stand-by ambulance was called out on to the track to pick up drivers dragged beneath overturned wagons, although it was subsequently announced over the P.A. system that neither man had suffered more than superficial injuries.

'The risk's all part of it,' said Sean when Toni expressed concern for those still waiting to race. 'It has to be spectacular or nobody would want to come and watch. Here, take the binoculars and keep your eyes on number four. He's going to win this next heat.'

Toni did so, but only for a moment or two, lifting upwards to casually scan the massed ranks of the grandstand across the arena. The glassed-in centre section had tables to one end, with people seated eating a meal while they watched the action below. Something familiar in the angle of a dark male head caught her attention, and she came back to the couple, lingered briefly, then slowly lowered the glasses.

'Did you say Rafe had a business meeting?' she said.

The words were almost drowned by the roar of the crowd as the race got under way. Sean was on his feet with the others about him, craning his neck to watch the wagon take the first bend at breakneck speed, then swinging round to be ready for them coming out of the back stretch which could not be seen from this position. His face, under the white stetson which matched the one he had bought her, looked young and alive, his mouth formed into a yell of encouragement for his favourite number four. Toni tried to register the same enthusiasm as the first wagon thundered into view, followed closely by its team of outriders, but her heart wasn't in it. Her enjoyment of the day had taken a decided tilt downwards.

'Said he'd do it!' Sean crowed as number four passed the winning post a good wagon length ahead of his nearest competitor. 'Wouldn't be surprised if he took the final.' He subsided back into his seat, turning his head as if in sudden realisation. 'Did you say something?'

Toni kept her voice casual. 'Only that your brother's business associate seems very attractive. He's up there in the clubhouse with a redhead. I suppose it's what you could call a working breakfast.'

'Where?' Sean took the glasses from her, training them on the expanse of glass.

'Third table, second row down.' All Toni could see at present was that two people were seated there, but the position was fixed in her mind. 'She's wearing a pink fringed shirt and a neckerchief.'

'Got them.' Sean brought down the glasses from his eyes with a curious expression. 'That's Audrey Cooper. I didn't know Rafe was seeing her. She's only just twenty.'

That much Toni had judged for herself. The girl looked every inch the bright young Canadian. If Rafe was using her as an escape valve then he should be ashamed of himself. She was much too young for a man like him.

'Who is she?' she asked, still striving to appear relatively detached.

'Her father owns a ranch north of here. Biggest in the area. It joins on to Surewater land.'

Toni glanced at him sharply, sensing something behind that statement. 'Another ranch?'

'Rafe's. He inherited it from his mother's side. He has a manager to run it for him.' His tone was thoughtful. 'Maybe he's considering selling out to Don Cooper after all. Don's been after him to do it long enough.'

'He'd hardly be discussing that kind of deal with the man's daughter,' she pointed out, then paused as another thought struck her. 'Unless he's planning another kind of merger.'

'No way.' Sean's tone was decisive. 'He'll never marry while my mother's still alive. She won't let him.'

'She might have to if he once makes up his mind. Perhaps he's pandered to her up to now because he hasn't felt strongly enough about anyone, but I can't see him doing it for the rest of his life. Some time he has to forget about feeling responsible for the way she is and make a stand.'

He was silent for a moment or two, looking at her strangely. 'Not with Audrey,' he said at length. 'She'd never marry a man fourteen years older.'

'Why not?' Every word was a self-inflicted injury, but she made herself go on. 'Plenty of girls that age fall for older men. You saw the two of them up there—the way she was looking at him.'

'You're imagining things,' he came back flatly. 'She wasn't looking any way at all.' They had both been speaking in low tones, conscious of the people about them. Now he grinned, deliberately lightening his mood again. 'There's still a whole lot to come. How about a long cool drink?'

Toni stayed where she was while he went to fetch them, the binoculars idle on her knee. To look again at the two in the stand would be tantamount to spying, yet the temptation was there.

Finally she could resist no longer, and swung the glasses up to her eyes. Rafe was easy to find; his face seemed to leap at her out of the crowd. He was watching the semi-final at present in progress, his expression reflecting little real involvement. Only when the girl at his side leaned forward to say something to him did the lean features come alive, his mouth curving in a smile as he turned his head to look at her.

She was worth smiling at, Toni acknowledged numbly. Young, pretty and quite obviously adoring. What man could resist such a wealth of charms?

CHAPTER SEVEN

Sean's number four wagon took first place in the final as he had predicted. Blindly watching the antics of the arena clowns which preceded the bareback riding, Toni finally acknowledged the truth. She had gone along with what Sean had asked of her for one reason and one reason only—because to do otherwise would have meant never seeing Rafe again. Yet what good had she hoped it might do in the long run? If there had been enmity and suspicion in Rafe's mind before there was even more now, and she could hardly blame him for it. She had done everything possible to implant it there.

So far as she could see, she had three alternatives. She could walk away from the whole Stewart family—disappear without explanation; she could stick it out as she had promised Sean until he considered himself capable of retaining the initiative he had grasped, or she could go to Rafe, confess the whole thing and ask his help on Sean's behalf. No course appealed, the last least of all. At best he could only regard her as interfering in the affairs of his family, and that was hardly likely to enhance her character in his eyes. And what of Sean himself? She had given him her word that she would see him through, at least for a week or two. Foolish perhaps, but there it was. She had been foolish all the way through this affair.

It was lunchtime before the last of the bareback riders had taken his turn at the eight-second ordeal. Cramped from the long session on the hard, narrow seats, Toni was only too ready to move when Sean suggested they go and get some food. Without the glasses, she could not be one hundred per cent sure that Rafe and his companion were still at their table, although someone in a dark-hued shirt like the one he had been wearing certainly was. In any case, she reasoned, the chances of bumping into one couple in such a crowd were very slim.

Had she known that the restaurant for which Sean was making was in the Clubhouse itself she might not have felt as confident. It was only when they reached the head of the escalator and she saw the signs directing the way to the Clubhouse seats that realisation came, and by then it was too late to suggest a different venue.

'Suppose we see your brother?' she murmured, and drew a suspiciously bland glance.

'Suppose we do? We've as much right to be up here as he has—probably more, considering he's not in the least bit interested in rodeo.'

In which case his attendance must be purely in the interest of his lovely companion, Toni reflected. Lucky girl to have found a man willing to make such concessions. Lucky girl all round, in fact. She had looked so happy, so lacking in complication. There was no way a girl like that would ever get herself mixed up in the kind of mess she, Toni, was in at the present moment. She would have more sense.

The eating areas were to the rear of the concourse. Sean was first to spot the two for whom he was obviously looking, drawing Toni with him as he made for the table.

'Mind if we join you?' he asked as Rafe looked up. 'Save breaking up a larger party.'

It was the girl who answered, her face lighting with a smile. 'Hi there! Of course we don't mind.'

It was difficult to read anything in Rafe's features. Toni avoided his eyes as he made the introduction, but something in his tone must have got through to Audrey somehow, for her smile faded just a little.

'I didn't know,' she said. 'Congratulations, Sean. You too, of course, Toni. When do you plan on getting married?'

'We haven't talked about it yet,' Sean put in before Toni could answer. 'I guess not too long. How are your parents? I haven't seen them in ages.'

'Not since you came out to Surewater last fall,' she agreed. 'They're fine, thanks.' The blue eyes came back brightly to Toni. 'You must find things very different from England.'

'Yes, I do.' That was one question she could answer with truth, Toni thought. She went on quickly before the next obvious one could create difficulties. 'You live a far more outdoor life here. At home the weather can change from one hour to the next, so there's always an element of doubt attached to any outdoor activity.' She sounded stilted, she knew, but she couldn't help it. Sitting next to a silent Rafe she found it impossible to relax and be herself.

'If you're going to live here you'll have to start thinking of Canada as home,' said Audrey with faint asperity. 'After all, it will be, won't it?'

'I suppose you're right.' Toni forced a smile, and hurriedly changed the subject. 'Sean was telling me earlier that your family has a ranch north of town.'

'Earlier?' It was Rafe who had spotted the slip, his tone sharpening.

'We saw you through the glasses,' Sean admitted airily. 'Purely by chance. It must be years since you last came to the Stampede.'

The reply was brief but succinct. 'It is.'

'Tell me how you and Sean met,' put in Audrey, obviously aware of some atmosphere if not the cause of it. 'I guess it must have been recently.'

'I looked after the horses out at Copper Lake for a few weeks,' said Toni, passing over the latter question. 'Just a temporary job until the regular man got back.'

'Copper Lake?' Audrey's brow wrinkled for a moment, then cleared. 'Oh, that must be the place you were telling

me about last time you came out home, Rafe. First of a
chain, didn't you say?'

'Providing the odds come out in our favour.' He was
looking at his brother, mouth tilted. 'There's every chance
now that they might.'

'He means because it doesn't depend on my efforts any
more,' Sean explained without apparent rancour. 'There's
every chance he's right. I can't say my heart was in it.'

'If you like to ride, Sean must bring you out to Fire
Creek,' said Audrey before Rafe could form any cutting
remark. 'You'll have a whole string to choose from.
Maybe we could plan an overnight camp. I haven't done
that in ages. Rafe, you'd come, wouldn't you?'

'Unlikely,' came the reply. 'I can't afford the time.'

'One night?' She pulled a face, playing up the disappointment. 'Surely you can find that much.'

His smile and shrug were noncommittal. 'Maybe. Did
you want any dessert?'

She took the hint, shaking her head. 'I expect it's time
I got going. We've a run-through at two. I'm with the
Young Canadians,' she added for Toni's benefit. 'We're
in the show each night along with all the rest. I hope
you're going to come and see it.'

'Not tonight,' said Sean before she could answer. 'We
have other plans made.'

'You wouldn't get in anyway. It's a total sell-out. Try
for midweek. We should have ironed out all the problem
spots by then.'

'We'll make it,' promised Toni. 'You can be sure of it.'

'Great. I'll be counting on a good report next time I
see you.' Audrey got up along with Rafe, her glance flicking to Sean's face with an expression which in other
circumstances Toni might have described as wistful. 'I
hope you'll both be very happy.'

Rafe's leavetaking was briefer: a nod of the dark head
and he was gone. Toni sat back in her seat and looked at

Sean with stormy eyes.

'You did that deliberately. Why?'

His shrug was a parody of his brother's. 'Just curious.'

'And was your curiosity satisfied?'

'No.' Suddenly the nonchalance had flown. 'No, it wasn't. But I know one thing. If Rafe does anything to hurt that girl I'll——' He let the sentence peter out as the waitress came up with their order, avoiding her gaze. 'Let's eat, shall we?'

The place had filled up, and a queue was forming along the concourse. Although nothing was said, one felt bound to hurry through the meal in order to give others an opportunity to eat. Inside half an hour they were ready to go.

'Feel like sampling what the Midway has to offer?' asked Sean on the way down to the ground level. 'You'll need a strong stomach for some of the rides, but they're great fun!'

Having seen something of what he was talking about, Toni privately doubted that latter statement. Being spun upside down and inside out on a space-age fairground machine was not her idea of fun.

'What about your mother?' she asked. 'She's been on her own all morning. Surely some member of the family should go and spend a little time with her.'

'She isn't alone. She has Eva.'

'Eva?'

'Guess you didn't meet her yet. She sees to all my mother's needs—a bit like a personal maid. She's a qualified nurse too, so she's well able to cope.'

'It wasn't just coping I was talking about. Don't you spend any time with her yourself?'

'Not much,' he admitted. 'We don't have a lot in common. She has a specially adapted car she can drive. She isn't confined to the house. Rafe takes her places when he's home. She prefers his company anyway.' His glance was defensive. 'You think I'm making excuses, don't you? Well, I'm not. Any time we do have together she spends comparing me with Rafe. I've been a disappointment to her all my life. That's why——' He broke off abruptly, shook his head. 'Forget it.'

'That's why you grabbed the opportunity to take a dig at them both, through me,' she finished for him softly. 'You do live just for the moment, don't you, Sean.' It was a statement, not a question. 'How do you think she'll react when this so-called engagement of ours breaks up?'

'I don't know.' He sounded depressed. 'Maybe I'll just walk out at the same time.'

'And do what?'

'I don't know that either.' He made a wry little gesture. 'I'll have to think about it, won't I?'

There had never been a better time for plain speaking, Toni decided. 'Yes, you will,' she said. 'You can't be a failure all your life.' She gave him a smile to take some of the sting out of the words, and nodded towards the main doors. 'We could be at the house inside an hour.'

Sean spoke very little on the way, all his attention seemingly concentrated on the road. He had been expecting more support from her, Toni knew, but he wasn't going to get it. Not any more. She was only just beginning to realise how immature he really was. Jealousy of Rafe was only part of it. He had no drive, no ambition. She had provided him with an excellent excuse to abandon his role out at Copper Lake.

How she was going to handle the situation from here on in she wasn't yet sure. If Rafe had his way she would not be here long enough to handle it at all. Rafe. Her throat closed up at the thought of him. If she had any real sense she would get out now while the going was good. Last night's threat had not been an idle one; he had meant every word. To stay here in the face of it was a challenge in itself. At least, that was how he would take it. Yet she knew that a voluntary leavetaking was beyond her. For the present, at any rate. Anything was better than total deprivation.

It was a surprise to find Rafe's car parked in front of the house when they arrived. Sean reacted in obvious disgust.

'We needn't have come back after all. He should have said!'

'I don't suppose it occurred to him,' Toni defended automatically, and drew a sour glance.

'Meaning he'd hardly expect me to have the same idea? Neither would I have had if you hadn't forced it on me. Anyway, I'm not spending the afternoon with the two of them together. I'm going back to town. Coming?'

Toni looked at him for a long moment before slowly shaking her head. 'I'm staying.'

'Suit yourself,' he said, and got back into the car, turning in a tight circle to speed down the drive in the direction of the gates.

She watched him go with mixed feelings, aware that he would probably not return for the evening either. Which left her alone with the rest of the family. It was a daunting prospect, but one which had to be faced. Only not just yet. She needed an hour or two to herself first.

She made her room without seeing anyone. The balcony doors had been opened, with the screen left closed against any marauding insect life, admitting a pleasant little current of air. Karen's voice came up clearly from the poolside below:

'You're sure it was Sean's car?'

'As sure as I can be from the engine noise. I didn't see it.' A scraping sound of metal against concrete, then Rafe spoke again. 'They must have changed their minds and gone back to town.'

'Buy why?' Karen sounded puzzled. 'Why come all this way just to do that?'

'Who knows?' (In her mind's eyes, Toni could almost see the shrug.) 'That son of yours isn't a creature of logic. Maybe they had a row and he left her and then changed his mind when he got here.'

'Did they seem at odds when you saw them?'

'No, but he didn't like my being with Audrey. Worked out better than I hoped. I thought we might have to go looking for them.'

There was a momentary pause before Karen spoke again. 'Audrey's a sweet girl. I'm not sure you should be using her this way.'

'I'm not doing anything she wouldn't do for herself if she knew the way things were. She fell hard for Sean when he spent that week at Surewater in the fall. I can't think why—he isn't at all her type. He liked her too, though.'

'Not enough to do anything about it.'

'That's Sean, isn't it? He needs pointing in a given direction. Our English friend recognised that much early on. Given the encouragement, Audrey is capable of asserting herself.'

'You intend telling her, then?'

'At the right time.' Another pause, then he added on a different note, 'Karen, she'd be good for him. Young she might be, but she's got backbone. Wouldn't you rather see him married to a nice Canadian girl?'

The answer was a long time coming. 'I guess so. Anyone except this Toni.' Karen hesitated briefly. 'You never really said just how attractive she is—that beautiful hair, and those eyes. Enough to make any man want her.'

'Want, maybe.' His tone had hardened again. 'Trust is something else. I wouldn't believe a word she said.'

'Getting rid of her might not be so easy.'

His laugh came low and harsh. 'Don't worry about it. By the time I'm finished with Madam Brentwood, she'll be glad to go!'

Toni forced herself into action, sliding the double-glazed door along as quietly as she could manage it. Not that she should be the one to worry if they heard her. Quick angry tears stung her lids for the brief moment it took her to dash them away with a fierce little gesture. Eavesdroppers rarely heard good of themselves; why should she expect anything different for herself? Those two down there were of a kind.

What hurt most was Karen Stewart's hypocrisy. Lulling into a sense of false security, she believed was the term. Well, forewarned was forearmed. Neither Rafe Stewart nor his stepmother was going to decide her actions for her. She would play them at their own game—starting right now!

It took her only moments to find a swimsuit and put it on, drawing it up the length of her slim, shapely body with a sense of purpose. 'Want, *maybe*,' Rafe had said down there. Her first aim would be to remove any doubt. Let Karen watch and yearn. She deserved no better!

With her hair fastened up in a swathe on top of her head, Toni seized a short robe and put it casually about her shoulders, then took a look in the mirror, trying to see herself through a man's eyes. She had what it took, according to all she had heard and read. The question was, could she put it to deliberate use and still remain inviolate herself? There was only one way to find out.

A plain-featured woman in a white uniform dress and shoes was coming up the stairs as Toni descended. The quick shift of expression across the other face made her wonder just how far Karen confided in her nurse. She paused and smiled, holding out her hand.

'You must be Eva. We didn't get to meet last night. I'm Toni Brentwood.'

'Yes, I know.' The tone was pleasant enough, but the handshake simply a touching of fingers. 'I thought you and Mr Sean were still in town.'

'He is—at least, he'll be part way back by now. He dropped me off. I'm not used to all this heat.'

'Oh, I see.' From the blankness in her voice, Eva saw not at all. This was obviously not how engaged couples acted in her experience. Toni could almost hear her deciding that there had been a quarrel of some kind. She wasn't so far wrong either.

'I'm on my way out for a swim,' she said, somewhat unnecessarily considering her appearance. 'Are Mr and Mrs Stewart still out there?'

'I think so. They were ten minutes ago for sure.'

'Okay, thanks.' Toni ran on lightly down the stairs, aware that the woman was gazing after her. A qualified nurse, Sean had said, yet that didn't have to mean looking like one. Toni found it surprising that Karen could stomach the constant reminder of her incapacity in the sight of that uniform. Unless that reminder was for Rafe's benefit—although one would have thought the wheelchair alone was more than enough.

No more concern about that side of things, she reminded herself hardily. From now on she treated as she found. A wheelchair gave no one the right to make decisions governing another's life. That was something Karen had to learn. As for Rafe—— She let the black anger rise just enough to give her incentive, controlling it behind a determined façade. He would learn too, but in a quite different way.

The two of them were sitting by the pool, Karen on a long, angled lounger with her legs stretched out beneath a gaily patterned skirt. She was wearing a sun-top, her shoulders smoothly tanned above it. On her feet she would be about five feet six, with a figure in near perfect proportion. In spite of everything, Toni was unable to stifle a momentary flash of sympathy. Such tragedy shouldn't happen to anyone.

The sight of Rafe was enough to harden her heart

again. He sat in a chair with feet propped comfortably on the front rail of another, his back bare and bronzed, dark head arrogantly poised. A glass half full of ice and some unidentifiable liquid stood close to hand on a wrought-iron table. As Toni moved towards them, he lifted it to his lips, taking a long pull before setting it down again.

Karen was the first to see her, the muscles in her neck standing out clearly as she tensed in surprise. Toni took the initiative from her with a wide bright smile.

'Hi there. Do I need a swim! This has to be the hottest day yet!'

Rafe swivelled to look at her, feet dropping to the ground. His recovery was fast, his glance upwards to the balcony overhead swift in comprehension.

'So Sean went back to town without you,' he said.

'That's right.' She leaned her weight against the table edge and gave a philosophical little shrug. 'We had a slight difference of opinion—nothing important. He'll be back.'

It was Rafe who answered, face expressionless. 'You sound very sure of yourself.'

'Oh, I am. It doesn't do to be otherwise.' Toni was laughing as she said it, making a joke of the words in full knowledge that he was not in the least amused. 'That's something else we share—Rafe.'

The use of his name, soft and deliberate, brought a spark to the grey eyes. She was only feet away from him, legs stretched out and crossed at the ankles, hands behind her supporting her balance. The robe had fallen open above the tied belt, revealing the outline of her breasts under the thin material of her suit. She saw his gaze drop as if without volition, heard Karen's indrawn breath and knew no shame at her behaviour. Stirring this man physically was all she cared about: making him remember what it had been like before. He had wanted her then and he would want her again, but he would never have her. She was going to show him just how that felt.

'I'm going to take a dip,' she said. 'Are you coming?'

She didn't wait for any answer, but pushed herself away from the table to slide off the robe and drop it casually to the floor. Walking to the poolside, she stood poised for a moment, arms lifted in a pretence of securing her hair, then with one swift movement she dropped them level and dived into the water.

She swam the length before surfacing, smoothing the water out of her eyes as she turned. Rafe was sitting where she had left him, but there was nothing relaxed in his attitude. He said something to Karen in a short aside, then rose to his feet, shoulders broad and powerful above the tapering length of his body in the black trunks. Despite his size, he cut the surface with scarcely a splash.

Heart beating suddenly faster, Toni waited for him to reach her, slinging both arms backwards along the edging rail in support of her body and kicking idly with her legs in apparent unconcern. When he surfaced it was almost immediately in front of her, thrusting back his hair from his face with a gesture she might have found intimidating had they been entirely alone.

'How much did you hear?' he demanded, treading water to keep himself upright.

'Hear?' She widened her eyes at him in questioning surprise. 'About what?'

'You know damned well what!' His voice was low but dangerous, the jerk of his head towards the house indicative of a tight control. 'You were up there a few minutes ago, weren't you?'

'Well, yes.' She let her own gaze move upwards to the windows of her room. 'But sound doesn't travel through double-glazing. I'd have thought you'd know that.'

He eyed her for a narrowed moment before swivelling to follow her gaze, taking in the closed door beyond the balcony with a faint contraction of his jaw. 'It was open earlier.'

'Then someone must have closed it,' she returned with sweet logic. 'All I did was change. Anyway, your business secrets would have been perfectly safe. I doubt if I'd have known what you were talking about.'

He didn't believe her; she could see that in the way he looked at her. Not that it mattered a great deal. She hadn't expected him to do so. Her smile was slow.

'Poor Rafe, always so suspicious! Why don't you relax a little? We could still be—friends.'

The slight hesitation on the last was not lost on him. She saw him stiffen for a moment, but only for a moment, then the control was back. His lips thinned into a smile of his own.

'Maybe we could at that.'

Hooked, she thought in satisfaction. She had his interest. Sean could take a back seat when it came to indulging his baser instincts. He deserved putting down for that alone.

'Come and have a cool drink,' he invited. 'Karen will be going up for her physiotherapy soon.'

Toni was surprised and showed it. 'Does it do any good?'

'If you mean does it give her any chance of ever walking again, the answer is obviously no. It helps keep what muscular usage she still has in good shape.' He grasped the rail across the corner, holding himself lightly upright. 'Every day for fifteen years. It's a boring routine, but she never misses.'

'Not even when she's ill?' Toni met his glance blandly. 'Sean mentioned she sometimes is.'

'She suffers pain from time to time.' His tone was short. 'A broken back doesn't necessarily mean total lack of feeling. Are you coming for that drink?'

'Sure.' She pushed off from the side with a strong backwards kick of her feet, passing close enough to him to feel the brush of his thigh against her hip. If Karen hadn't been watching she knew he would have grabbed hold of her; she sensed the instinctive reaction in him.

He passed her before she was halfway to the other end of the pool, hauling himself out and standing up to extend a hand to her when she got there. Toni saw Karen's face through the V of his legs and knew the older woman liked none of this. She steeled herself not to weaken, smiling into Rafe's face as he drew level.

'Thanks. I'll have a Tequila Sunrise if you can manage it.'

'I'll do my best,' he said with mockery. 'Did you want a towel for your hair?'

'That's all right. I'll leave it pinned up.' She took the seat he had recently vacated, lifting her feet to the same position and leaning back with an audible sigh of content. 'This is the life!'

Rafe looked at Karen. 'Would you like something?'

She shook her head. 'Eva will be coming for me shortly. But don't let that stop you.'

Toni wondered if Rafe too had noted the faint brackishness in the last. If he had he gave no sign of it. He disappeared indoors through the sliding screens which gave access to a large sun lounge. There was a bar across one corner. From where she sat, Toni could see him take out clean glasses and start to mix ingredients.

Karen was the first to speak. 'Did Sean say what time he might be home?'

'No,' Toni admitted.

'So the quarrel was rather more serious than you gave us to understand a few minutes ago?'

'It wasn't a quarrel at all,' she explained patiently. 'He wanted to do one thing and I wanted to do another. We both have a right to a free choice.'

Karen seemed to digest that for a moment before responding. 'You really believe he had a right to walk out on you that way? You don't mind him not caring enough to sacrifice his time to pleasing you?'

It was Toni's turn to be silent for a moment while she considered her reply. Karen was talking about herself, she realised—about her own relationship with her son. What she said now might be crucial to Sean's future welfare.

'I don't think anyone has a right to demand sacrifice from anyone else,' she said slowly at last. 'If it's made at all it should be voluntary. Sean doesn't necessarily think any the less of me because he didn't want to spend the afternoon lazing around. He'll come back all the sweeter for having gone his own way.' She hadn't meant to say the last, but it struck a good note. She only hoped Sean would not let her down when he did return.

Rafe came back with the drinks, putting a stop to any response Karen might have found. His glance went thoughtfully from one to the other of them, as if he sensed some conflict.

'Five minutes,' he said, 'and we'll get you into the chair ready for Eva. Think you'll make it down to dinner tonight?'

'Of course.' Her tone was abrupt. 'I usually make it, don't I?'

It was not a question which required an answer, and Rafe didn't attempt one, taking a seat on the edge of a nearby lounger. The eyes briefly meeting Toni's were impassive. If he recognised the tension he was not responding to it.

'Had an idea we might go out to Surewater next week-end, invite some people over for a barbecue lunch on Sunday. A change of scene would do you good, Karen. You haven't visited the ranch in almost a year.'

'I'll think about it,' she said, still on a short note. 'Depends how things go. Sean may have other plans.'

And his presence was vital, of course, thought Toni dryly, or how was Audrey going to work on him? The rancour that had carried her through the last half hour had somehow dissipated. She felt suddenly weary of the whole affair, Rafe included. Sean had to release her from her promise, and he had to do it soon. There was no way she could keep up this pretence until he decided enough was enough.

CHAPTER EIGHT

Eva's arrival was a relief. Watching Rafe lift his step-mother in strong arms to deposit her in the wheelchair standing ready close by, Toni wished she had kept her mouth shut a minute or two back. It wasn't up to her to tell any member of this family how to run his or her life. They had to sort out their own problems.

It was a simple need of something to say which brought the question to her lips as the two women vanished indoors. 'Did you never think about using the pool for some of these therapy sessions? I understand water exercises can be very beneficial in a lot of cases.'

'Karen has a phobia about anyone seeing her legs,' Rafe came back levelly. 'Apart from Eva, that is. The pool is too public.'

'Surely it could be kept private for half an hour a day?'

'Not to Karen's satisfaction. Do you think it hasn't been tried?'

She was doing it again, Toni realised wryly. When would she learn? 'I'm sorry,' she said. 'I should have known.'

His eyes narrowed a fraction, as if he found the apology suspicious in itself. When he spoke again it was on a harder note. 'What exactly did you say to her?'

'When?' she asked, playing for time.

'You know when. While I was fetching the drinks. You could have cut the atmosphere with a knife when I came out again.'

She sighed and gave in. 'I spoke out of turn.'

'About what?'

'Sean. We were discussing the sacrifice of personal free-dom for reasons of loyalty.'

'And you naturally were against it.'

She refused to drop her gaze. 'I'm against any pressure being brought to bear. Loyalty has to be earned, not taken for granted.'

'And you think that's what Karen does?'

Toni stirred restlessly, aware that non-involvement was not all that simple to achieve. 'Can we talk about something else?'

'Sure.' His tone was deceptively mild. 'As good friends we can discuss any topic under the sun. Name your choice.'

'Rafe.' She said the name hesitantly, not quite certain how to set the record right between them. 'What I said in the pool a while ago——'

'Talking about me?' asked Sean from the other side of the closed screen doors. 'The Prodigal Son returned to the fold!'

'You're mixing your metaphors,' returned his brother, barely turning a hair. 'If you'd come a little earlier you could have spent a few minutes with your mother—or didn't that fit in with your plans?'

'Not with you there too.' He paused, still making no attempt to open the screens. 'Toni, can I have a word with you?'

'You can come out here and have it,' cut in Rafe before she could answer. 'I'm going up to change.' He got to his feet, his glance sliding over her face with a look she found disquieting. 'We'll finish our discussion another time.'

It was he who slid open the screen, holding it back pointedly until Sean had come through, then closing it again behind them.

'What did he mean?' asked Sean when he was out of sight and earshot. 'What discussion?'

'He was just being funny,' she said, and wished she could believe it. She looked at him questioningly, taking in the sheepish expression. 'Get it out of your system?'

'Some,' he agreed. 'I realised I was being unfair to you leaving you here on your own to face my family. Not that you seem to have been doing too badly.'

It was not how Toni would have described the happenings of the last hour or so, but Sean wasn't to know that. He had seen her and his brother apparently holding a close conversation and put his own interpretation on it. She had no intention of telling him the truth of the matter. It might be enough to put him against Audrey altogether, and that would hardly be kind to the girl who knew nothing as yet of Rafe's plans for her.

'It's a matter of opinion,' she said and hesitated before tagging on slowly, 'Sean, I really think we should call it a day. My being here isn't doing you any good.'

'How can you tell?' he demanded. 'It's barely been twenty-four hours. If you leave now you'll be breaking your word.'

'I'm asking you to release me from it.'

'Well, I don't. Not yet.' He made a gesture of appeal. 'I have to have someone on my side.'

'It wouldn't be so bad,' she returned, 'if you knew what you were fighting for. If you don't want to work within the Company, then you have to have some other alternative mapped out. What about photography on a professional basis?'

His shoulders lifted hopelessly. 'Starting with what? I don't have control of any capital.'

'That doesn't have to be the end of it. Who is executor for the estate until you're twenty-five?'

'My mother.'

'I see.' Toni bit her lip, aware of having blundered. 'Well, that needn't stop you from trying. Executors have the legal right to advance from capital under certain circumstances—at least, they have in England, and I shouldn't think it's any different over here. Why not put it to her? If she saw you were enthusiastic about it she might consider it worth backing. Getting some professional to endorse your work could help to persuade her.'

Sean looked unconvinced. 'Not a chance.'

'You can't be sure without trying. Even if you fail you'll at least have made some effort.'

He was silent for a long time, considering her. 'I'll think about it,' he said at length.

It would be too easy to leave it there, Toni decided. Sean didn't just need pointing in the right direction, he also required keeping there. 'Rafe suggested everyone spending next weekend out at Surewater,' she said with purpose. 'If you haven't done something about organising your future by then I shall leave anyway, so think about it hard, Sean.' She got up then, reaching for her robe and sliding it about her shoulders. 'I'm going in to wash my hair and change. Are you going to be here for supper?'

'I guess so,' he agreed moodily. 'No reason why we shouldn't go out later on, though. There's an all-comers party just a few blocks down the road if you don't fancy going into town again.'

Toni hesitated, torn between the need to be out of Rafe's way if he planned staying in for the evening and reluctance to further the lie they were living. Finally she compromised.

'I'll come, providing you introduce me simply as a friend of the family staying for a short time,' she said. 'I'm taking it that your brother is hardly likely to be there too?'

'No.' Sean shrugged resignedly. 'Friend of the family it is. Don't dress up. It's still Stampede gear.'

But not jeans, she thought, making her way indoors. At least, not for her. She was tired of looking Western.

It took her some time to brush-dry her hair after washing it, curling the ends softly under about her face and thanking Providence for the natural wave which made

perms and rollers unnecessary. By the time she had
finished it was already gone six-thirty. With the tan she
had acquired out at the Lake, she had little need of make-
up apart from a dab of lipstick and the faintest touch of
eye-shadow. That done, she got into a cotton skirt in pale
tan together with a drawstring-necked blouse in white
which managed to look appropriately casual yet feminine
at the same time. A pair of tan canvas sandals completed
the ensemble.

Rafe was coming out of the room a couple of doors
down from hers when she emerged at ten minutes to the
hour. It was the first time she had realised that he was
so close. It gave her a feeling of insecurity she had to
fight to keep from showing as he waited for her to reach
him.

'Planning an evening out?' he asked, viewing her appearance with mocking appreciation. 'Let me guess. The
Mason barbecue?'

'If that's just a few blocks down the road, you're
probably right,' she said. 'Sean didn't tell me the name of
the people.'

'It's them okay. Their Stampede parties are legend.'

Toni kept her eyes front as they moved towards the
stairs. 'Shall you be going?'

'Would you like me to go?' he countered. 'Or do you
think Sean might object?'

She looked at him, then, a swift assessing glance which
told her little. 'Rafe——' she began, and stopped
abruptly, realising there was no way she could explain
her behaviour in the pool earlier without admitting that
the reason for it lay in what she had overheard. The
temptation was strong in her to break down there and
then and tell him the whole truth. It would hardly be
likely to enhance her character in his eyes, but at least she
would be free of the burden of deceit.

She didn't because she couldn't, too conscious of the

light in which it would also show Sean. They had reached the gallery now. Rafe paused, looking down at her with enigmatic eyes.

'Rafe—what?' he queried softly.

'Just a passing thought,' she said. 'Aren't you coming down?'

'I usually bring Karen down with me.' If he had noted that she was ignoring his previous question he was apparently not about to pursue the subject. 'Gives Eva chance to get out the night table before she eats. She likes things organised.' His glance went beyond her and hardened. 'Just in time to see your fiancée down to supper—providing you're both planning on eating here at all?'

'Yes, we are.' Sean moved into view from the doorway of his room, looking as reluctant as he obviously felt. 'Not my choice, I can tell you.'

'That I wouldn't doubt.' The grey eyes came back fleetingly to Toni. 'Seems we have you to thank for getting the family together for once. Karen will be grateful.'

Sean drew in an angry breath as his brother walked off along the gallery towards the door at the far end next to the elevator. 'Can't let an opportunity pass,' he remarked bitterly. 'I've half a mind to leave right now!'

'If you do I'm not coming with you,' said Toni firmly. 'That was aimed more at me than you. He thinks I manipulate matters to my own ends.'

'Better than having him manipulate you to his,' he reminded her on a note which brought a faint flush to her face.

'I hadn't forgotten. It's the whole reason I'm here. Let's go down, shall we?'

Karen spoke little during the meal, but her presence was there to be felt. Watching her covertly from time to time, Toni wondered how she combated the sheer sameness of her days. To live one's life seeing the world from a sitting position could hardly fail to give a narrow viewpoint. She needed taking out of herself, given some interest beyond home and family. Occupational therapy meant more than basket making and such. There must be many ways in which an intelligent person could utilise their time.

'I never asked you if you enjoyed the Stampede,' said Karen at one point, catching her eye. 'What you saw of it, at any rate.'

'I thought it great entertainment,' Toni replied truthfully enough. 'More dangerous than most of the riders made it look though—and especially the wagon racing.' She paused before tagging on casually, 'Do you plan on going down yourself, Mrs Stewart?'

The other shook her head, smile perfunctory. 'It's hardly my kind of thing.'

'I was thinking more of the show at night,' Toni confessed. 'I understand it's usually very good.'

'It's usually excellent,' Rafe corrected, not unpleasantly. 'I tried to persuade Karen to go and see it last year, but she wasn't interested. Maybe you can talk her into it this year.'

'Why don't we all go together?' Toni responded, accepting the challenge without hesitation. 'Midweek, didn't Audrey say? We could perhaps have one of those tables on the very top row, then there wouldn't be any problem.'

'There wouldn't anyway. Wheelchairs are catered for. How about it, Karen?'

She looked at him without expression. 'I'll make up my own mind, I don't need anyone's help.' Her gaze came back to Toni, losing nothing of its coolness in the process. 'You'll be meeting Audrey again at the weekend if you come out to Surewater. The Coopers are next-door neighbours. You do plan on coming, don't you?'

'I don't remember being asked,' put in her son before Toni could answer, and drew a quelling glance.

'You weren't here when it was discussed. I'm sure Toni would welcome the change.'

'Yes, I would.' She said it with firmness, daring Sean to balk any further. 'I've never been on a proper ranch before.'

'Surewater isn't all that large,' said Rafe, sounding relatively unmoved by his stepmother's remonstrance. 'Fire Creek has three times the area of land.'

'Why Fire Creek?' asked Toni, taking her cue.

'It's self-explanatory. The hillside overlooking the creek is covered in Jack pines. It takes a very high temperature for the cones of that particular species to split and germinate, so there has to have been a huge fire at some time in the past for the trees to grow *en masse*. Hence the name. I'm sure Audrey would be delighted to tell you more.'

Toni held the grey gaze without flinching. 'I'll remember to ask her.'

It was gone nine when they finally started out for the party. Sean's few blocks turned out to be more a matter of miles, cutting north of the city to a residential suburb of large, individually designed houses set in landscaped gardens. The Mason home was long, low and luxurious, the driveway curving around the front of the house to a parking area already full to overflowing. Regardless, Sean managed to tuck in his two-seater, conveniently ignoring the fact that in doing so he was blocking off all means of exit for at least three other vehicles.

Voices and laughter came from beyond the shrubbery to the rear. Cutting through it, they came out on to a wide expanse of lawn and flags with a floodlit swimming pool set obliquely across the middle. There were people everywhere, standing, sitting, jumping in and out of the pool in appropriate dress. Long trestle tables held enough food to feed an army, with two portable barbecues smoking at one end. Everyone looked to be having the time of their lives.

In the following half hour, Toni met so many new faces she lost track of names. Not that it really mattered, she told herself, as she probably wouldn't be meeting any of them again. At some point she lost sight of Sean altogether, finding herself drawn into a friendly argument on the relative merits of the Western versus the English saddle with a group of fellow riding enthusiasts. One of them, whose name she had heard only as Mick, turned out to be Audrey Cooper's brother, in town for the weekend and obviously intent on making the most of every minute. He was perhaps a year or so older than Sean, with Audrey's auburn tinted hair and blue eyes and a laughing, open countenance that appealed.

'Guess I should be at the show watching her debut right now,' he admitted cheerfully. 'Only this seemed more my line of country. The parents are there anyhow, so she isn't going on unsupported by family. Are you coming out to Surewater next weekend? Rafe hinted he was thinking of holding a Stampede barbecue of his own on the Sunday when I saw him this morning. Should be good. He never does things by halves. I had a real surprise seeing him with Audrey in tow. I always thought it was Sean she liked. Rafe's a great guy, but he's way out of her league.'

'If you object to him seeing her, why don't you tell him to leave her alone?' Toni suggested, tongue a little in cheek.

'I might if it were anyone else but Rafe. She's safe enough. He'll let her down lightly. He's known her since she was a baby. How long are you going to be staying at the Stewart place?'

'It depends,' she hedged. 'Over the next week, at any rate.'

'Then you're sure to be coming out to the ranch.' He sounded genuinely pleased about that. 'I'll be looking forward to next weekend.'

Someone else claimed his attention just then, and Toni found herself momentarily alone on the fringe of the crowd, the glass in her hand still more than half full of a fruit punch that hit one right between the eyes after a few sips. Delicious but dangerous, she thought now, taking another cautious taste. Lord only knew what was in it!

There was a table close by. Toni put the glass down on it and moved in the direction of the shrubbery, feeling the need for a few moments of peace and quiet. A path led down through formal flower beds to a small round summerhouse lit only by moonlight at present and surprisingly unoccupied. Once inside, the noise from the party seemed remote. Seated, Toni leaned her head against the wall at the back and closed her eyes. Just five minutes, then she would go back and rejoin the fun. They were a grand crowd of people and she enjoyed being with them. If only it could have been in a different way from this! She was here under false pretences.

The shadow falling across the doorway was more sensed than seen—a presence felt. She opened her eyes swiftly and sat up straight, unsure of who the newcomer was until a shaft of moonlight fell across too-familiar features.

'Sean desert you again?' asked Rafe with soft insinuation. 'That's really too bad of him. Maybe I can make up for his lack of attention. That's what you wanted, wasn't it?'

Toni came slowly to her feet, the edge of the wooden seating hard against the back of her knees. 'I made a mistake,' she got out. 'I tried to tell you earlier. I was angry and upset and I wanted to get at you in some way. That's all it meant.'

His expression didn't alter. 'Because of what you overheard?'

'Yes.' There was little point in denying it now. 'I did have the window open, just as you thought. I heard every word. Do you really believe you have the right to interfere in Sean's affairs this way?'

'His affairs are his own business, marriage affects the whole family.' He said it softly but with emphasis. 'I'm out to stop it, any way I can.'

She knew then that she was going to tell him the truth, Sean or no Sean. He might despise her even more than he did now, but at least they would have things straight.

'You don't have to go to the trouble,' she said. 'I never had any intention of marrying your brother. We're not engaged at all. It's a pretence.'

There was no judging his reaction. 'Why?'

'On Sean's part?' She made a small wry gesture. 'He needed a bolster.'

'Against what?'

'You—and his mother. He feels pushed into a corner. Dependent on you for everything.'

'Dependent on his mother. She's executrix for the estate.' The words were clipped. 'How was a mock engagement supposed to help?'

'I'm not all that sure myself. I think he hoped you'd both realise he had a mind of his own where his future is concerned. We planned to fake a break-up at an opportune time.' She searched the strong features for some sign of belief, sighing when she failed to find it. 'Rafe, I'm telling you the truth. Ask Sean if you doubt it.'

'You've told me why Sean did it,' he said after a moment, 'but you haven't explained your own part.'

Toni bit her lip, realising how far she was going to have to go to convince him. 'I'd have thought it obvious. I was hurt and I wanted to hurt back. Making out I'd been playing you along until Sean got back was the only way I could find of doing it.'

'You mean your pride was hurt.'

'Not just my pride. It went deeper than that.' She forced herself to carry on. 'I believed you were beginning to feel something of what I felt for you. Finding out it was all a sham was the worst thing that ever happened to me.'

'Not all a sham.' The smile held irony. 'It might have started out that way, but I kept losing sight of the main object. The other night at the lake, I was ready to believe I'd made a mistake. I planned on coming over early in the morning and talking it out with you.'

'Then you saw Sean and that was that,' she finished for him painfully. 'Rafe, I'm not trying to find excuses for what I did, but——' She stopped there, shaking her head in dull acceptance. 'They're just words, aren't they? I've no way of proving I mean them. It all boils down to the same thing in the end—lack of trust. You took Craig Shannon's word against mine from the start. If you believe me now you have to accept that he's a liar. Is that so impossible?'

'I guess not. He had his marriage to think of.' Rafe studied her for a moment as if trying to penetrate her thoughts. 'You must have given him *some* encouragement. Even Craig would need that.'

'If I did it was without meaning to.'

'You weren't attracted to him?'

'No. Well, not really.' Seeing his expression change, she could have bitten off her tongue. Sometimes one could be too soul-searching. 'He's a good-looking man,' she added quickly. 'I had to be aware of it. But that was all. I didn't want him making love to me.'

'Because he's a married man?'

'Not only that. There's a difference between finding a man attractive to look at and being attracted. I can't explain it any better. Another woman would know what I mean.' She paused hopelessly, knowing she was making little impression. 'It's no use, is it? I'm not going to convince you no matter how I try.'

'Maybe not with words,' he agreed. 'There are other

ways.' He came to her then, taking hold of her by the waist to pull her against him, his hands hard and hurting. 'If I'm different, show me how I'm different.'

Toni gave herself up to doing just that, letting go of any hold on her emotions and feeling the response in him. His hands brought her closer, moulding her to him in a manner that left no doubt in her mind of his own desire, his mouth hardening to a passion that seared.

It was Toni who broke away first, knowing it was now or never. 'Not this way,' she said thickly. 'I don't want it to be this way, Rafe. You have to trust me first.'

He was breathing hard with the effort of control, eyes narrowed to twin blazing points. 'Then make me,' he said. 'Give me reason to trust you.'

The appeal was dragged from her. 'How? I don't know how!'

'You'll find a way.' His hands came up to cup her face, holding her tightly so she couldn't look away from him. 'I want to believe in you, Toni. If I find out you've lied to me about you and Sean I'll hurt you worse than you've ever been hurt!'

'I haven't. You only have to ask him.' The words came without volition. 'Rafe, I love you. That's the truth too!'

He was silent for what seemed an age, expression hard to define. 'If I accept that,' he said at length, 'where do we go from here?'

'I don't know that either. It has to be up to you. If you tell me to go I'll go.'

'And if I ask you to stay?'

'I'll do that too.' Toni hesitated before saying it, aware that she was treading on delicate ground. 'You can't spend the rest of your life making up for something that wasn't even your fault in the first place.'

His jaw hardened abruptly. 'You don't know what you're talking about.'

'I do. Sean told me.' Having come this far she couldn't

bring herself to back down. 'I understand how you must feel, but you've done your part. Karen has to let you go.'

His laugh jarred. 'Would you like to tell her that?'

'No,' she conceded, 'I wouldn't like it. But I'd do it if I had to. It isn't as if she'd ever be left alone.'

The grey eyes took on a new expression. He said slowly, 'You really think any woman I married would accept that kind of situation?'

'Some.'

'Would you?'

Her heart jerked. 'Knowing the circumstances, yes, I would. She isn't a vindictive person. She just needs to learn that nobody can ever pay for what happened to her.' She paused irresolutely. 'Rafe——'

'It wasn't a proposal,' he denied dryly, 'just a hypothetical question. We should be getting back to the party.'

'To find Sean?'

'Why not? No time like the present.' The pause was calculated. 'Not afraid of the outcome, are you?'

'I don't have any reason to be.'

'In that case, let's get to it.'

The party was still going strong; that was apparent the moment they reached the main arena. Not so surprising, Toni realised, catching a glimpse of Rafe's watch as he raised his wrist to glance at it himself. They had been gone only a matter of half an hour, but it felt much longer. The man at her side was watching the crowd milling about the poolside, his profile austere. She ached for the touch of his hands again, the feel of his mouth on hers. Once Sean had verified her story everything would be different. She only wished it didn't have to depend on him.

It was several minutes before they found him. More accurately, he found them, weaving his way across the lawn to where they stood and throwing an arm about Toni's shoulders with laughter on his lips.

'I've been looking for you all over the place. Where'd

you go?' He seemed to notice his brother for the first time, his face losing some of its animation. 'Well, look who's here! Since when did you go in for this sort of thing?'

'Rafe wants to talk to you,' Toni said swiftly, side-stepping the arm. 'He knows about us, Sean.'

Hazel eyes moved from one to the other of them, taking on a sudden enlightenment in the process. Watching him, Toni saw his jaw go tense.

'Knows what about us?' he asked in an ominous manner. 'We don't have any secrets, do we?'

'You know we do.' She tried hard to keep any note of entreaty from her voice, aware of the listener at her side. 'I'm sorry for letting you down, but I couldn't keep it up any longer. I told him the truth.'

There was no change in his demeanour. His face had gone blank. 'I don't think I understand. He already knows we're going to be married. What else is there?'

'Stop it, Sean!' Her tone was sharp, rising to anger. 'It was never real, and you know it!'

'It was to me.' He managed to make the hurt sound genuine. 'Toni, why are you doing this to us?'

She gazed at him in dismay, unable to believe he could possibly be serious. 'Sean, please—don't try to pay me out like this. Tell Rafe the truth!'

'He's heard it.' The statement was flat. 'I'm sorry if it doesn't fit with any new plans you might have made, but that's how it is.'

'He's lying.' She made the appeal to Rafe directly, heart sinking at the hardness in his eyes. 'If it were true we'd have made some announcement here tonight, surely?'

'Except that you didn't want me to tell anyone just yet,' Sean put in, without fear of contradiction this time. 'I guess I should have realised there was something wrong.' He looked at his brother, mouth stretched to a thin line. 'Satisfied?'

'For the moment.' Rafe didn't even glance at Toni. 'I'll leave you to sort it out between you.'

Toni made no attempt to stop him as he walked away across the grass. It would have been a waste of time anyway. Chest tight, she turned back to Sean, seeing the defiance slowly fade under her gaze.

'Why?' she asked. 'Why did you do it?'

'Because I wasn't going to let Rafe take over, that's why,' he came back defensively. 'Anyhow, I did you a favour in the long run. He'd only make you miserable.'

'I'm miserable now,' she pointed out, and thought what an understatement that was. 'It wasn't up to you to decide what's good for me.'

'I did it because I care about you,' he protested. His voice took on a note of appeal. 'Toni, don't walk out on me. I need you.'

Her laugh was short. 'You really think I could stay here after tonight? You think Rafe is going to let me stay?'

'It doesn't have to be up to him.'

'It will be.' A tremor ran through her. 'So far as he's concerned, I lied to him. He isn't going to let that pass.'

'There's still nothing he can do if I want you to stay. And I do.'

'I'm sorry,' she said. 'You've made it impossible.'

'Oh, God!' He sat down suddenly on the grass, resting his forehead on his bent knees in a manner that made her wonder if he was feeling the effects of too much punch. 'I don't know what came over me, Toni. I've never done anything as rotten as that in my life.' His voice was muffled. 'Do you want me to go after him?'

She sat down beside him, resisting the urge to put a sympathetic arm about his shoulders. It was sympathy that had got her into this in the first place. That and stupidity.

'It wouldn't work,' she said dully. 'He'd just think I'd talked you into it. If there's a seat available on tomorrow's flight out I'll take it. Will you get me out to the airport?'

'If that's what you want.'

'It isn't a case of what I want, it's more of what I have to do. Can't you understand that much?'

'I guess so.' Sean lifted his head again, but slowly as if it might drop off should he jerk it too hard. 'I've had too much to drink and it's starting to catch up on me. Do you think you could drive us home?'

It was one place Toni didn't want to go, but she had nowhere else. Her things were there anyway. 'I'll manage,' she said. 'Do you want to go now?'

'In a moment or two, when I feel able to stand up.' His glance was rueful. 'I wish you'd let me talk to Rafe.'

She shook her head. 'It wouldn't be any use. Forget it, Sean.'

'I can't forget it.' He sounded desperately unhappy. 'You're in love with him, aren't you?' He didn't wait for her answer. 'I guess it was realising it just now that made me do what I did. I couldn't stand the thought of him taking what was mine.'

'Except that I wasn't and he hasn't,' she came back gently. 'I don't belong to anybody. Do you feel able to make it to the car yet?'

'With help. My head's going round in circles.'

Mick Cooper detached himself from a group around the swimming pool and came over to where they sat, squatting on his haunches to view Sean with a knowledge-able eye.

'Feeling bad?'

'And some,' agreed the object of his scrutiny. 'I don't know what Matt used in that punch, but it's sure lethal!'

'I guess he's not all that sure himself. He keeps tossing in another bottle in passing.' Mick looked at Toni with a smile. 'Need any help?'

'If you could give him a hand to the car,' she said, 'I'll drive him home.'

They made it unnoticed by all but a minority, drawing a friendly jeer or two when it was realised what the trouble was. With Sean seated safely if still not too happily in the passenger seat, Toni slid behind the wheel, smiling up at their helper.

'Thanks.'

'Any time.' He added cheerfully, 'See you at the week-end. I saw Rafe not so long ago and he told me you'd definitely be there. We could take a ride, maybe?'

'Maybe,' she agreed, not about to argue the point. He must have seen Rafe before the latter had followed her to the summerhouse. ''Bye, Mick.'

Sean fell asleep before they were halfway back to the house. Fortunately the route was simple to follow. Toni drove with concentration, trying not to think of what lay ahead. If Rafe had gone straight home he might very well be waiting for her.

The place was in darkness when she finally got there. She parked the car close to the main doors and shook Sean awake.

'I'm okay now,' he assured her, standing unsteadily upright when she opened his door. 'A night's sleep and I'll be as good as new!' He attempted to smile. 'Thanks for the lift.'

With visions of having to ring the bell for entrance, Toni was relieved to find the door unlocked. She refrained from taking Sean's arm during his shaky progression across the hall and up the stairs, sensing his embarrassment over the whole episode. Outside his door she said a whispered goodnight and carried on to her own room, closing the door behind her without switching on a light and leaning against the wood for a moment in order to gather herself together.

'Thinking about how to get out of this one?' asked Rafe from the shadows over by the bed. 'I can save you the trouble. You don't.'

CHAPTER NINE

SHE could see him as her eyes became accustomed to the darkness created by the drawn curtains. He was seated in the chair near the base of the bed, his whole demeanour one of waiting.

'You've no right to be in here,' she said, and heard the shake in her voice without surprise. 'Anything you have to say can wait till morning before I leave.'

'What I have to say is going to be said right now,' he came back hardily. 'I told you what would happen if you lied to me.'

'So what do you plan on doing?' she queried on a note of bravado. 'Beating me?'

'Nothing so crude.' He came to his feet, menacing in his size. 'You said you loved me, so now you can show me how. We're going to spend the night together.'

'No, we're not,' she denied, determined he wasn't going to make her crawl. 'I didn't lie, and Sean is ready to verify it now.'

'After you worked on him? Pity you didn't have time before. Sean would roll over and play dead if you told him to!'

'You neither of you have too much regard for the other, do you?' Toni responded with scorn. 'The loving brothers!'

'Half-brothers,' Rafe corrected, unmoved by the outburst. 'And whoever told you attack is the best means of defence has never found themselves in quite the same situation. I'm going to have what you promised me in the summerhouse tonight. All that passion shouldn't go unsatisfied. Get undressed—I'll wait that long.'

'Rafe, stop this!' Her voice came out husky. 'What do you think you're going to prove?'

'Not a thing,' he returned. 'I'm out purely for satisfaction. Given the right incentive, I'm sure you'll provide it.'

She gazed at him, breathing hard and fast. 'You're wrong. I won't provide anything. Whatever you do you'll be doing on your own!'

His smile mocked her. 'We'll see. Are you going to get your things off, or do I do it for you?' His move to grab her was swifter than hers as she turned to open the door. 'No, you don't! You're not running out on me.'

'Leave me alone!' She hit out at him as he pulled her towards the bed. 'Rafe, listen to me!'

'I already did.' He pushed her down on the cover, kneeling over her to peel off his shirt with a purpose that froze her. 'Don't worry, I'm not going to rape you. You're going to be warm and willing when it does happen—if it takes me all night to get you that way!'

It would take far less than that, and they both knew it. Even now Toni could feel the stirring inside her. She could tell herself she detested and despised him, but her senses failed to recognise that fact. She went limp, acknowledging the futility in struggling. Physically incapable of resisting him she might be, but she wouldn't lift a finger to help him.

If he had been cold and ruthless about it himself she might have succeeded. The soft, sensuous touch of his lips undermined her defences in a way no demanding pressure could have done. Her response was involuntary, her body relaxing to accommodate him as he came down over her.

He kissed her into total, mind-blanking hunger, his mouth following the passage of his hands over her body, finding every nerve, exploring every sensation. She heard the low, gasping moans coming from her own throat and could do nothing to control them.

Rafe was breathing hard too, but he hadn't lost control. He proved that when he lifted his head to look at her, mouth cruelly curved.

'Do you want me to go on?' he asked softly. 'Tell me, Toni. Let me hear you say it.'

Far gone as she was, some faint premonition filtered through, freezing her into stillness under him. The words came thickly. 'Rafe, don't.'

'Say it!' He hadn't raised his voice but the inflection cut like a whip. 'Tell me you love me now, you lying little devil!'

'I do.' She put a hand each side of his face, holding him fiercely as she looked into the grey eyes. 'It doesn't matter what you do to me, you won't change that! Ask Sean again. He'll tell you the truth.'

It was Rafe's turn to be still, gazing back at her with the struggle clearly reflected. Then quite suddenly he was gone, rolling away from her to lie on his back looking up at the darkened ceiling.

'You're driving me crazy,' he said through his teeth. 'I can't even think straight any more!'

'How do you think you've affected me?' she said shakily, lifting herself to an elbow. 'I always believed being in love was supposed to be a wonderful, happy experience, but most of the time you go out of your way to make me hate you instead.'

He rolled his head to look at her, no softening of expression in his eyes. 'If I'm such a bastard, why don't you?'

'Because I fell in love with the whole man, not just the bits I like.' Anger seared through her, tensing her throat muscles. 'The trouble with you is you want too much. Even if I could make you believe me over Sean, there'd be something else. Every bit of evidence you have against me depends on someone else's word. Why not try taking mine for a change?' She made a hopeless gesture at the lack of response from him. 'Damn you, Rafe. You can go to hell!'

His hand came out to her arm as she sat up, pulling her round and down again to the hardness of his chest. The kiss was savage, hurting her until she wanted to cry out, but she took it, waiting for the fierceness to run its course before attempting to lift her mouth away from his.

'You were right,' she whispered through bruised lips. 'You are a bastard! I must be crazy too.'

'I'll half kill Sean when I get hold of him,' he swore softly, still holding her. 'Why did he do it?'

'Because he's jealous of you,' she said. 'Not just over me, over everything. A lot of it's your own fault too. You don't try to understand him. It's you and his mother on one side and him on the other. How do you expect him to react?'

He studied her for a long tense moment, his hands hard at her back, then relaxed suddenly with a faint sigh, mouth taking on a rueful slant. 'You don't sound much like a woman in love.'

'I told you, I love you the way you are, not because you're kind and gentle.' She put out a finger tip and touched his lips, feeling the firmness give a little. 'Rafe, leave Sean alone, will you? He was feeling rotten enough about things when I got him home.'

'He deserves to,' came the short reply.

Watching him, Toni gave a sigh of her own. 'You're still not sure, are you? I don't suppose I should blame you too much. Craig Shannon did too good a job.'

'What would you do if you ever met the Shannons again?' he asked with an odd inflection. 'Would you tell Diane the way things really were?'

She shook her head. 'What point would there be? The way Craig is she'll find him out sooner or later without being told.'

'I've an idea she already suspects,' he admitted. 'He's never been able to resist an attractive woman.'

'Then why did I get all the blame?'

'Because he got to you before I did and you were the only one available to take it out on.'

'That doesn't sound very fair.'

His smile came faint. 'You just got through telling me I'm anything but. In any case, I meant what I said earlier. You must have given him some reason to think you'd be willing, knowingly or not. Those eyes of yours promise a man all kinds of things.'

'Then I'll have to start wearing dark glasses.' She felt her insides turn liquid as she looked into the dark features. Any moment now he was going to turn her under him again, and then she would be beyond making any decisions of any kind.

His hold tightened when she started to move. 'Where do you think you're going?'

'Just far enough away from you to keep some sense of proportion,' she said. 'We're here like this for all the wrong reasons, Rafe. It has to be different.'

'You mean you want me to tell you I love you before we make love?' There was cynicism in his voice. 'It's only a word.'

'Not to me it isn't. It mightn't be to you either if you'd let yourself feel.'

His eyes had narrowed to her face, seeking something deeper than the surface. When he spoke again it was in a different tone. 'Just how much did Sean tell you about the way Karen is?'

Toni hesitated, not quite sure how far she dared go. 'He said she became ill the only times you ever brought a girl home to meet her,' she said carefully at last. 'If either one had meant enough to you would you have held out?'

'I'm not sure,' he admitted. 'The question didn't arise.' He was still looking at her; still searching. 'When I knew Karen was a paraplegic, I gave her my word I'd always take care of her. It doesn't matter whose fault it was. I was driving the car.'

'Looking after her doesn't have to mean going without a life of your own.'

'I haven't,' he said. 'I've simply kept the two separate, that's all. So I was wrong. I should have made things clear from the start. At nineteen it's difficult to see that far ahead.'

'Especially when you're riddled with guilt,' she agreed softly. 'Rafe, even if the accident had been your fault you couldn't have done any more. You've a right to your own life.'

His hand came up to touch her face, a smile faintly etching his lips. 'With you?'

'If that's what you want.' Her heartbeats were unsteady. 'Only you'd have to be totally sure about me first, and you still have doubts, don't you?'

'Some,' he acknowledged. He studied her a moment longer, then made a sudden decisive movement to sit up, putting her away from him as he did so. 'You're right, it would only confuse the issue. I need to think things through.'

'Don't give Sean a hard time,' she begged. 'He had too much to drink tonight or he wouldn't have said what he did.'

'I'll bear it in mind.' Rafe stood up to pull on his shirt, mouth slanting as he looked at her. 'You're not making it easy.'

She pulled up the neckline of her blouse with unsteady fingers, wishing it only could be easy. Why couldn't she have fallen in love with some nice, uncomplicated man who would love her back without question? She knew she didn't mean that. Rafe was the only man she wanted.

He came to her, lifting her head with a hand under her chin, expression controlled. 'We'll talk tomorrow,' he said. 'Just be sure you know what you're doing, that's all.'

'I already am,' she whispered.

She stayed where she was for some time after he had gone, thinking about what had been said. If Rafe asked her to stay could she do it, knowing how far from ideal their whole relationship was? On the other hand, could she bring herself to leave and never see him again? If the choice was offered she doubted if she would have the strength of mind to make it the latter.

Trapped, she acknowledged ruefully. Emotions were the devil.

It was late when she finally slept, and gone ten when she woke. Sean was sitting out by the pool alone, his damp hair testifying to a recent swim. He looked round on her approach, his smile more than a little strained.

'Hi,' he said on a subdued note. 'Did you eat?'

Toni shook her head. 'I'm not hungry, thanks. I need to clear some cobwebs.'

'If you're going in for a dip I'll have some coffee brought out,' he offered, stirring himself. 'Or tea if you'd rather.'

'Coffee sounds good.' Her tone was forcibly bright. 'I'll just do a couple of lengths to loosen up.'

She did several more than that, swimming with a slow, precise stroke that left her mind free to wander. Seeing Rafe again was going to be the most difficult moment. He was unpredictable, capable of having changed entirely from the man who had left her last night. In the cold light of day he might very well decide that what he felt for her was not enough to disrupt his whole life over. Toni doubted if it was herself. She was the only one who was in deep.

The coffee was ready and waiting when she eventually climbed out of the pool. Sean poured her a cup while she towelled her hair, pushing it across the table towards her as she sat down in one of the reclining chairs.

'Rafe took my mother for brunch with some friends,' he said. 'They won't be back till mid-afternoon. Is there anything special you'd like to do today?'

'Nothing I can think of.' She looked at him for a moment, trying to find a way of asking what she wanted to ask. In the end she just said simply, 'Did Rafe have anything to say to you this morning?'

'About last night, you mean?' The rueful look was back in his eyes. 'He told me to lay off the drink if I couldn't take it. I started trying to explain about—you know what—but he cut me off, said it wasn't important.'

'I see.' Her heart felt leaden. 'Well, that seems fairly cut and dried!'

'Toni, I'm sorry.' He sounded wretched. 'I'd give anything to be able to make things okay for you. If I'd realised before how you really felt about him——' he paused there, his mouth taking on a wry tilt—'well, I'm not going to make out I'd have been delighted, but I'd have reacted differently. The only thing I was really interested in was getting you back here with me. We were so close before he came along!'

'Only superficially,' she said gently. 'We were friends, Sean. Just good friends.'

'You let me kiss you,' he defended.

'Once. And only then because you did it at a time when I happened to be in need of a little comfort.' She softened the words with a smile. 'You're a great guy, to put it in the vernacular, but you need someone different. You know it too, deep down.' She paused dryly. 'You didn't like it when you saw Rafe with Audrey Cooper, did you? Did you stop to ask yourself why?'

'He's too old for her,' he said. 'That's why. She's just a kid!'

'She isn't. Twenty is fully adult.'

He was silent, digesting that, his face changing expression a little. 'You think she's really gone on him?' he asked at length.

'No, I don't. Any more than he's gone on her. They

just happened to be lunching together, that's all.' Toni
kept her tone casual. 'Why shouldn't they be? He must
have known her since she was a baby. Mick didn't seem
to find anything in it anyway.'

'Maybe you're right,' Sean said slowly. He met her
eyes and gave a sudden faint grin. 'You're right about
something else too. It was more than just the age thing. I
felt——'

'Jealous?' Toni suggested on a soft note as he hesitated.
'You don't have any reason to be. I got the distinct impression that you were the one she felt something about.
Didn't you see her face when Rafe introduced me as your
fiancée?'

'I was too livid to take much notice.' There was a
thoughtful look in his eyes. 'You really think she—likes
me?'

Her laugh was involuntary. 'If you had any vanity
about yourself at all you'd realise how easy it is to like
you, Sean. Audrey can't be the only girl attracted to you.
In fact, I know she isn't. I saw at least two more hanging
on to you at the party last night.'

'Probably because there was nobody else available.'

'There you go again!' This time she didn't smile.
'You're a very good-looking and attractive person. Why
can't you believe it? You never showed all this doubt in
yourself with me.'

'I never really felt it,' he said. 'You were so easy to talk
to. It was only wanting to impress you that made me
stand up to Rafe in the first place.' His voice took on a
new note. 'It got me out of a job I hated doing, at any
rate. From now on I don't get pushed anywhere.'

'Fine,' she came back dryly, 'providing you don't take
it too far. I imagine you were only put in charge of that
particular project because you needed some kind of involvement in the Company. You told me yourself it was
the only thing you showed any aptitude for.'

'Based on one season at the Valemount lodge, and that was already a going concern.' He shook his head. 'I'm not cut out for management in any form.'

'Then go out for independence. It might be a struggle for a couple of years if your mother won't realise any capital to you, but you could take a job in the same field and get some experience while you're waiting.'

'It might be worth thinking about.' He sounded intrigued by the idea. There was a brief silence between them before he said slowly, 'What do you plan on doing now, Toni? I guess I don't have any right to ask you to stick around any longer, but it's going to be difficult to explain if you suddenly up and go after a couple of days.'

'You mean because of your mother?' She looked back at him squarely. 'I think she should know the truth.'

He winced. 'I don't fancy the idea of telling her. She'll think I'm a total fool.'

'I doubt it. Not if you tell her why you felt moved to do it in the first place. It might even make her realise a few things.'

'It might.' His tone was doubtful. 'At least it would get it through to Rafe, too.'

If he believed it, Toni reflected with doubt of her own. Aloud she asked, 'Is there a London flight out today, do you know?'

It was a moment before he answered. 'I'm not sure. I'd have to check.' He made a restless movement. 'Toni, you can't go running off this way. What about Rafe?'

'What about him?' She kept her tone emotionless. 'I'll simply be saving him the trouble of seeing me off himself. It isn't just you, Sean. He doesn't trust me, period.'

'Because of Craig Shannon? That guy needs a punch on the jaw! I've a damned good mind to go down there and do it myself!'

'That wouldn't help anything.' She was smiling despite herself. 'Thanks all the same.'

'Rafe should have his brain examined,' came the disgusted response. 'I don't know how you can feel anything for him.'

'I'm a masochist,' she said without inflection. 'I fall for all the wrong men.' She caught his eyes and deliberately lightened her tone. 'Don't worry about it, Sean. I'll get over it. Just help me get away.'

'I'll do what I can.' He heaved himself to his feet, albeit with reluctance. 'Hang on.'

There was little else she could do, considering, she thought as he disappeared indoors. She saw him lift the telephone receiver from its rest on the bar and press out a swift sequence on the number panel. If there was no direct flight to London today, she could perhaps take one as far as Toronto and fly on from there tomorrow. An overnight stay couldn't cost a great deal, certainly not enough to make any great difference to her state of finances. A job was going to be a first priority. That, and somewhere to live, of course—although the Y.W.C.A. would serve initially. In a few weeks she would have forgotten all about this part of her life—might even have met a man she could really relate to.

She was kidding herself, and she knew it. Nothing about this affair was going to be forgotten. Put at the back of her mind, perhaps, but it would always be there waiting for an unwary moment. The outlook, to say the least, was not a rosy one.

Sean came back shaking his head and trying unsuccessfully to hide his lack of regret. 'Nothing before Wednesday. This time of year they're always busy.'

'What about Toronto?' she asked. 'Or even Montreal?'

'I've no idea offhand. Didn't ask.' He sounded disconcerted. 'You realise you could get stuck?'

'It's a chance I'm willing to take.' She half lifted herself to her feet when he failed to move. 'The airline can always check the position ahead for me anyway.'

'I'll see to it.' There was resignation in his voice. 'If you're so determined to go I guess I can't stop you.'

This time he was more successful, though not, according his expression, from his point of view.

'There's a Montreal flight at two,' he announced. 'And they can get you out on a London flight on Tuesday evening. Can you cope for two days?'

She would have coped with a great deal more in order to get herself on that plane. 'I'll go and pack,' she said by way of an answer. 'Luckily I never got round to taking all my things out of my case.' Her smile came faint. 'Premonition, perhaps. What time shall we have to leave for the airport?'

'Half after twelve.' Sean seemed about to add something else, then apparently changed his mind, shoulders slumping defeatedly. 'At least you'll have time to eat before you go.'

Toni doubted if she would feel like it, but made no comment. She would be gone from the house by the time Rafe returned to it, and that was all she cared about. If there were any lingering doubts in his mind as to the way he felt about her, her departure could only bring him relief. Remove the temptation and the problem solved itself, so to speak. That applied to her too, of course. She wished she could convince herself of it.

It didn't take her long to shower and change into a lightweight green trouser suit that would be comfortable for travelling. Packing away the few items she had taken from her case took even less time. She put the damp suit in a plastic bag and tucked it away in a corner without overdue concern. Wherever she stayed that night she could take it out again and dry it off properly. In the meantime it couldn't do much harm.

Sean had a light luncheon of cold cuts and salad ready and waiting for her when she went back down at eleven-thirty. She ate some of it to please him, and drank two cups of coffee to please herself, forgetting that caffeine could be a depressant as well as a stimulant. It was a relief when the time came to leave for the airport.

Sean was not talkative in the car; he seemed to have run out of things to say. Toni was grateful for the silence. Making conversation was a little beyond her at present. Once she was on the plane she would be all right. She had to be all right.

With her luggage unloaded on to a trolley outside the terminal, she told Sean not to bother parking the car, holding out her hand with a bright little smile.

'I'd rather say goodbye right here if you don't mind.'

'I do mind,' he said, but he didn't argue about it. His eyes held regret. 'I'm sorry, Toni. I was a selfish idiot bringing you here at all.'

'I was the idiot for coming,' she denied. 'Forget it, Sean. Just remember to stick out for what you really want.'

She turned away quickly, pushing the trolley ahead of her through the automatic doors and heading for check-in without a backward glance.

Seated in the departure lounge waiting for the flight to be called some twenty minutes later, she heard the announcement over the tannoy system with a philosophical acceptance. An hour's delay was not going to make so much difference, simply that much less time to wait at the other end. In the meantime another cup of coffee would help to pass it on.

By a quarter past two she was on her third, not so much because she needed the liquid but to occupy her hands and mind to a certain extent. So far the delay time was still holding, which meant they should be calling the flight within the next fifteen minutes or so. In another hour they would be in the air and heading east away from all this. Three days from now she would be back home in England ready to start her life over again. If that thought held little appeal right now it would then. She would make herself interested if she had to work at it night and day.

Automatically she moved over as someone slid into the seat next to her. From the corner of her eye she saw a hand take up the spoon from the saucer it had just placed on the table and stir slowly.

'You're not getting on that plane,' said Rafe with quiet emphasis. 'I just had your luggage taken off the transporter.'

Toni made no immediate movement. She felt confused. If Rafe genuinely wanted her to stay why had he left her so pointedly alone this morning?

'Why?' she got out.

'I'd have thought last night made that obvious.'

She looked at him then, taking in the steadiness of the grey eyes. 'Last night made only one thing obvious, and you didn't take advantage of it.'

His smile was faint. 'For reasons I explained at the time.'

'I know. That's why I thought you deliberately got out of the way this morning, to give me a chance to leave.'

'Afraid I'm not capable of that much subtlety,' he returned on a dry note. 'It was a long-standing engagement I'd forgotten about myself until Karen reminded me. I'd have left you a message, except that it never occurred to me you'd take things the way you did. I rang the airport to have you paged as soon as Sean told me where you were, then found it wasn't going to be necessary.' He paused there, glancing about him with drawn brows. 'We can't talk here. Come and reclaim your baggage and we'll do it in the car.'

She still made no move. 'Going where?'

'Back to the house. Where else?'

'As Sean's fiancée?' She shook her head. 'I'm through with all that, Rafe. Your stepmother deserves the truth.'

'She already knows it. I told her the whole story on the way home from the Lawrensons'.' His expression gave little away. 'She'll accept it because she has to. I made that clear.'

'Accept what?' Her voice was so low it was almost a whisper.

'That you're coming back for my sake, not Sean's.' He made a decisive movement to stand up, his hand coming under her elbow. 'We'll discuss it in the car.'

Toni went with him because she couldn't help herself, emotions in a whirl. For his sake, he had said, but how far did that go? If he didn't believe in her now he was hardly likely to do so in a week or two. In returning like this she could be laying herself open to the kind of heartache she would never forget, yet she was still doing it.

They headed in a northerly direction away from the airport, angling towards the ever-present mountains on a minor highway until all signs of the city were left behind.

'Surewater's about forty kilometres or so further on,' said Rafe, bringing the car to a halt eventually at the junction of a crossroads. 'We take a left here to get back to the house.'

He turned his head then to look at her, resting an arm along the back of the seat between them. His voice was rock-steady. 'Did you mean what you said about being prepared to take Karen as part of the deal?'

Toni gazed at him for a long moment without answering, seeing the clean-cut lines of his jaw, the firm mouth and straight jut of a nose, feeling the tension curling down deep as she came back to the grey eyes again. 'What kind of deal?'

'Marriage,' he said. 'I want you to marry me, Toni.'

Her breath felt trapped. It was too soon; too sudden. She couldn't accept that he meant what he said. Rafe watched her without moving, waiting for an answer she was incapable of producing. As usual it was impossible to tell what he was really thinking.

'So say something,' he urged with dry intonation.

'Why now?' she forced out. 'Last night you weren't sure about anything. Only this morning you refused to listen to what Sean had to say.'

'I didn't refuse,' he responded equably. 'I told him it wasn't important any more. I meant exactly that. If I'm going to accept you at face value then I do it wholesale.'

'No more doubts?'

'No more doubts.'

It was pressing too far, but she had to be sure. 'Not even over Craig Shannon?'

His hesitation was brief enough to be almost non-existent. 'Not in the way you mean. Craig's the type to need the message spelling out loud and clear. Maybe you just didn't freeze him off hard enough.'

'That might be true,' she conceded ruefully. 'It's difficult to know how far to go with that kind of thing. After all, he was my employer.'

'And in the past,' he agreed. 'Let's leave him there.' He put out a hand and slid it behind her neck to draw her to him, holding her there with his eyes on the soft fullness of her mouth. 'I want you,' he said on a sudden rough note. 'And I need you. I'm not going to let you say no to me, Toni!'

Want; need—every word except the one she wanted to hear. Yet wasn't it a good enough start? It had to be, she acknowledged in swift resolution, because there was no way she could turn down what Rafe was offering her. He could learn to love her. It was up to her to make sure he did. At least she would be fighting, so to speak, from an inside position.

She gave him her answer in her lips, responding to the demand in him without restraint on her emotions. He was breathing hard and unevenly when he put her from him, his eyes darkened.

'Don't tempt me,' he said. 'It's neither the time nor the place.' A smile touched his lips as he looked down into her face. 'This way you're totally transparent.'

Toni knew then that she still didn't have his trust. Not wholly. She told herself she didn't care. She had him, and that was all that mattered for now. The rest would come.

'Does Karen know?' she asked, striving to control her own unsteadiness. 'Did you tell her just why you were fetching me back?'

'I had to tell her,' he said. 'I wanted to give her some time to adjust to the idea.'

'You were that sure I'd say yes?'

The smile came again very faintly. 'I was that sure I wasn't going to let you say no. You've given me more restless nights than any woman I ever met before. The times I've imagined having you right there with me, seeing your hair spread over a pillow, the look in your eyes when you start wanting the way I want. I'm going to have all that—and more.'

Toni had her eyes closed, her senses tuned to the sound of his voice, the feel of his hand at her breast. 'You could have had all that without marrying me,' she whispered. 'If you'd stayed last night I couldn't have held out—and you knew it.'

'Except that once wouldn't be enough,' Rafe came back roughly. 'This way I know you'll be there when I want you to be there. Make no mistake about it, Toni, what's mine is mine only. I don't share in any sense.'

'I won't let you down.' She tried to underline the words, to make them sure and certain. 'I love you, Rafe. One day you'll believe it.'

'One day I might even understand the distinction,' he came back on a faint note of irony. 'For now I'll settle for what I can see and feel.'

His kiss was briefer this time, but no less searing in its intensity. He released her abruptly and reached for the ignition. 'Let's go home.'

Home. For the first time Toni allowed herself to think about what that was going to mean. Karen was part of the deal, Rafe had said, and she would be the last to argue the point. The question was whether Karen herself would be prepared to accept things the way they were. On the face of what Sean had told her, it seemed unlikely.

'Whose house actually is it?' she asked suddenly, and felt his glance.

'I wondered when that might occur to you. On the face of it, it belongs to Karen, although she only holds a life interest so she can't sell it or alter anything structurally without my say-so.'

'But she can ask you to leave?'

'Yes, she can do that. If she does, we'll live out at Surewater. It's only an hour into the city by car, and there's an airstrip right on the doorstep.'

She said it almost to herself. 'If Sean leaves too she'll be alone.'

'Apart from Eva.' His jaw had gone tight. 'We'll cross that bridge if and when we come to it. You were the one who told me I couldn't spend the rest of my life paying for what happened to her.'

And she was the only one to persuade Karen that nothing had changed, Toni acknowledged. Rafe wasn't lost to her; she simply had to learn to share him. She only wished she could persuade herself it was going to be easy.

CHAPTER TEN

Sean was coming down the stairs when they went into the house. He paused when he saw them, face reflecting a cross-match of emotions.

'So you got there in time,' he said unnecessarily. 'I'm—glad.'

'Thanks.' Rafe's tone was short. 'Where's your mother?'

'In her room.' The younger man seemed to steel himself. 'The doctor is with her. She had some kind of seizure right after you left.'

Toni's eyes were on Rafe's face, registering the sudden blanking out of all expression. It was happening again, just as before. Only this time it couldn't work—*mustn't* work! He had to break free of the hold she had on him.

'I need a drink,' he said with flat intonation. 'I'll be in the study. Let me know when he comes down.'

Toni made no attempt to follow him, waiting until the study door had closed behind him before speaking.

'How bad is it?' she asked Sean.

'I've honestly no idea,' he said unhappily. 'She just collapsed.'

'Genuinely?' Toni hated herself for saying it, but it had to be said. 'You don't think she could have been putting it on?'

'Not a chance. She was as white as a sheet when I lifted her up. I couldn't find a pulse at first!'

'But you think it happened because Rafe had told her he was coming after me?'

'Not wholly, no.' He sounded wretched. 'She tore into me after he left—said I was to blame for having brought you here in the first place. I guess I lost my head, I know

I said some pretty rotten things back. In the end I told her I was getting out too. I said she'd finish up a lonely old woman. I was halfway out of the door when I heard her fall.' He paused there, misery in his eyes. 'It's all my fault!'

'No, it isn't.' Toni made her tone forceful. 'If anyone is to blame, I am. I told you to stand up to her. If it weren't for me none of this would have happened.' Her eyes went beyond him to the man descending the stairs. 'Is this the doctor?'

It was a purely rhetorical question; the man's identity was obvious from the bag he carried. He looked professionally noncommittal.

'I think we should have the whole family together,' he said in answer to Sean's query. 'Did Mr Stewart get back yet?'

'He's in the study,' Sean replied. 'This way.'

Toni was out by the pool when Sean came to find her, having spent the intervening minutes imagining all the worst reasons why the consultation should be taking so long. He looked sober.

'Rafe would like to see you,' he announced. 'Will you go to him? He's still in the study.' He shook his head at the question in her eyes. 'I'd rather he told you. It isn't easy to explain.'

The study was a room Toni had not entered before. Book-lined and leather-chaired, it was an essentially masculine retreat, a place to be alone in when the pressure became too great. Rafe was standing at the window, his back to the room. He turned on her entry, expression controlled.

'It isn't going to work,' he stated flatly. 'I was a fool to think it might. I should have let you take that plane this afternoon.'

'What did he say?' Her voice was low.

'It doesn't matter what he said. The facts remain.'

Toni drew in a steadying breath, trying to treat this thing rationally. 'Only an hour ago you asked me to marry you. I think I have a right to know why you changed your mind. If your stepmother's illness depends on my staying or going then it can't be organic.'

'It isn't.' He said it without emotion. 'But it's no less real for it. The mind can take over matter where the incentive is strong enough—or that's what I'm given to understand.'

'You mean she wills herself to be ill and she really is?'

'More or less. It isn't necessarily a conscious act on her part. In some ways that makes it worse. The subconscious can't be reasoned with.'

'You could try,' she appealed. 'We could all try. She has to realise that both you and Sean have a right to live your own lives. All she needs is reassurance that she'll never be left alone.'

'That simple?' There was hard derision in the question. 'If the conviction is so great you don't alter it with a few words.'

'You might. It would surely depend on the words.' She wanted badly to go to him, but instinct told her this was not the time. 'At least let me talk to her,' she said. 'We haven't had the chance to even get acquainted. If I explained about Sean——'

'No.' The tone left no room for appeal. 'I'll see about fixing you up with a flight out tomorrow. Don't worry about anything. You'll be taken care of.'

Don't worry about anything, when her whole future was at stake! Toni wanted suddenly to laugh—hysteria, she realised. Karen had won after all. From now on Rafe was hers and wholly hers. He thought too much of her to risk putting her through the pain of his being anything else.

'You're wrong,' she said on a dull note. 'You're not doing Karen any good.'

'I'm not doing her any more harm, which counts more.' He made a weary gesture. 'Leave it alone, Toni. We'll both get by.'

'*You* will, no doubt. After all, I couldn't give you anything a dozen other women couldn't give you!' She was out to hurt, her body racked by a pain also emotionally based. 'The only difference will be that you won't have one quite so readily available!' Her voice broke, suddenly, catching on the lump in her throat. 'Rafe, I love you. Doesn't that mean anything?'

'It might be if I was totally convinced you meant it,' he came back with the same hard inflection. 'There are other men. You won't have any difficulty finding one. Maybe with a great deal more to offer too.'

She stared at him with darkened eyes, trying to re-concile the images of a couple of hours ago with the man who stood before her now. 'If that was all I really wanted why should I have tried to get away?' she asked huskily. 'I ran because I couldn't bear the thought of you telling me to go. You didn't have to come after me.'

'No,' he agreed, 'I didn't. Better if I hadn't. Wanting a woman is no adequate substitute.' He shook his head as she made to speak. 'That's all I'm going to say on the subject. It's over. You're going home.'

If home was where the heart is, she reflected dully, then hers would always be here. Further argument was useless. Even without Karen the whole relationship would have been doomed to failure.

She turned without another word and went from the room.

The bedroom she had occupied these last two nights had its blinds half drawn against the sunlight. She opened them again in order to step out on to the balcony, leaning on the rail to view the far landscape with dispirited eyes. Tomorrow she would be gone for good, that scene out there lost to her for ever. It was only a minor part of her heartache, but it counted. She could have loved this coun-try, as she loved one of its people. Now she would never have the chance.

The knock on the outer door was too tentative to give any hope that it might be Rafe having second thoughts.

She called 'Come in' and moved indoors as Sean obeyed the invitation.

'Thought you might need some things,' he said, dropping her suitcases to the floor. 'I'm not above the occasional sweated labour!'

'I'll only need enough for overnight,' Toni returned, seeing no point in keeping it from him. 'I'll be leaving in the morning. Thanks for the thought, though.'

'Just an excuse,' he confessed. 'I'd an idea Rafe was going to react this way. I could see it coming when Don Conlin was saying his piece.'

It was a waste of time going over it, but Toni asked the question anyway. 'What exactly did he say, Sean?'

'He suggested a psychiatric hospital, but Rafe wouldn't hear of it—said he'd find his own solution.' He looked at her with sympathy and compassion. 'Guess he did just that. Not that I think he's right.'

Her shrug belied her depth of feeling. 'It hardly matters who's right and who's wrong. He made up his mind. As short a time as I've known him, I doubt if you or I or anyone else but your mother herself is going to change things now. I agree with him too. I don't think psychiatry is the answer.'

'She is emotionally disturbed,' Sean pointed out.

'Yes, but the cause of it is pretty obvious. Did anybody ever really try to talk to her about the future, or have you just left it to her to imagine what might happen should you and Rafe find outside interests?'

'I guess we might have, at that.' He sounded disturbed himself. 'I never thought about it that way before.'

Then it's time you started, Toni was about to say. She stopped herself because it was futile to labour the point. Whatever happened, it was too late now for her. Rafe wouldn't change his mind. When it came right down to it Karen held the only power to move him.

She said slowly, 'Sean, would you do me a favour?'

'Anything I can.'

'Go and ask your mother if she'll see me. Tell her I'm leaving in the morning and I'd like to say goodbye.'

There was doubt in the hazel eyes. 'I don't really think——'

'Trust me,' she appealed. 'I wouldn't do or say anything to harm her. I'd just like the chance to tell her that things aren't the way they seem.'

The doubt was still there, but he nodded. 'I'll try. I can't promise anything, though. If she's developed one of her headaches she won't be seeing anybody.'

Toni sat and waited his return with a mind made purposely blank. Useless to try and plan ahead on what she might say to the older woman should the opportunity be given her. She would have to play it by ear, trust to her senses to tell her how far she should go. Win or lose, at least she would have made every effort she could to free Rafe from his self-imposed chains.

She knew as soon as she saw Sean's face that it was no use hoping.

'I couldn't get past Eva,' he confessed. 'She says Mother's under sedation and not to be disturbed. Sorry, Toni.'

She shook her head in bleak repudiation. 'It was probably a lousy idea to start with. Don't worry about it, Sean.' Her smile was purely for his benefit. 'Do you think I might have some tea up here? I'm dying of thirst!'

'There's the rest of the day to get through too,' he returned with some shrewdness. 'Are you coming down to supper?'

'I'll be there.' It would be hell to sit across from Rafe knowing it was for the last time, but Sean was right, she couldn't stay in this room until it was time for her to leave. 'Don't worry,' she repeated. 'It will be all right.'

The afternoon wore on slowly. She forced herself to drink the tea when it came because it seemed churlish to send it back untouched when she had asked for it, yet the normally refreshing brew tasted bitter in her mouth. The accompanying sandwich she left completely alone. Her hunger was not for food, it was for Rafe; for the feel of his arms about her, the sound of his voice in her ear, the hard comfort of his body trapping her with its weight— all the things she would never know again. Other men might come into her life, but they could none of them ever equal Rafe. It was a soul-destroying outlook.

She was early down for supper because she could no longer bear the solitude of her room. Fixing herself a drink at the sun-lounge bar, she took a seat close by the screens and sat with the untouched glass in her hand looking out on the rippled surface of the pool. There was a storm gathering, she thought; one could feel the electricity in the air. The last one had been out at the lake, the night Rafe had told her their future relationship was in her hands. She wasn't in love with him then, but it hadn't taken long. And now she was leaving, going back home. Except that it wasn't any longer. She belonged right here with him. She always would.

He came in a moment or two later, casually clad in slacks and a long-sleeved shirt open at the neck. He made no comment when he saw her, mixing himself a dry Martini and bringing both shaker and glass across to a chair a few feet away from her own.

'You're on the eleven o'clock flight to Toronto tomorrow,' he said unemotionally, 'and the London one on Tuesday. I didn't think you'd be too keen on moving far, so I booked you into an airport hotel for the night. Okay?'

'Thank you.' She tried to keep her own voice level. 'Do you think I might have a cab to collect me in the morning?'

'Could be best,' he agreed. 'I'll see to it first thing.'

There was a silence after that. He didn't look at her, leaning back in the chair with one knee lifted across the other and a total lack of expression on his features. Toni let her eyes drift over him hungrily, remembering the feel of him, the scent of him, the sheer overwhelming maleness of both mind and body. When she spoke it was in direct defence against her longing to go to him.

'How do you intend living your life from now on?' she asked.

'The same way I lived it before,' he returned.

'Keeping your women away from the house?' She gave him no chance to answer, hand curled tightly about her glass. 'I'd settle for that if that's all there was.'

'But I wouldn't.' This time he did look at her, face taut with an emotion not so far removed from anger. 'Just leave it alone, will you, Toni.'

'It would be better than nothing,' she insisted on a desperate note. '*Any*thing is better than nothing!'

'Not for me it isn't.' His tone was unrelenting. 'Maybe it's as well this happened. The odds were against it working out anyway.'

'Why?'

'It hardly matters now. You're getting on that plane tomorrow. If there's any doubt about it I'll see you on to it myself.'

'That won't be necessary.' Pride gave her all the control she needed. 'I'll go without a struggle.'

There was little conversation over the meal, none of them being disposed to make the effort of dissemblance. Looking up during one such lull, Toni found Rafe watching her with cynicism in his eyes, and had the sudden feeling that he might even be grateful for having the decision taken out of his hands. Wanting a woman was no adequate substitute, he had said earlier, and he had been right. Physical need was only part of what she felt for him. Without the rest his own need of her would not have lasted long.

'I'm going for a ride,' he announced as soon as they finished eating. 'Want to come?'

The temptation was strong in her, but she resisted it. To be alone with him now could only make things more difficult.

'No, thanks,' she said. 'I'll stay here with Sean.'

The latter was the first to speak after his brother had left the room. 'I'm going to hate this house when you've gone,' he stated flatly. 'I'm going to do as we talked about and find myself a job.'

'Your mother——' Toni began, and saw him shake his head.

'It's Rafe she's really scared of losing. He's done more for her than I ever did. She could accept it when she believed I was the one you were marrying, but not when it came to Rafe.'

'You're wrong,' said Toni. 'She didn't accept it. She only pretended to because she knew there was a good chance it wasn't going to last. It was no accident that we saw Rafe with Audrey Cooper at the Stampede. They planned it between them.' She was watching his face as she spoke. Now she added quickly, 'Audrey knew nothing about it. She was simply the bait to pull you out of my clutches.'

There was anger in the hazel eyes. 'They had no right to use her in that way!'

'No, they didn't. On the other hand, I think they were right in thinking she had a lot more to offer you than I could. She's a lovely girl, Sean.'

'I know she is. She always has been.' He said it almost fiercely. 'Just let him go near her again, that's all!'

'There's one sure way——' Toni started to say, and broke off abruptly as the door opened again, gazing at the newcomer with a mind gone suddenly blank.

It was left to Sean to put the question, his tone revealing a concern he for once made no attempt to hide. 'What is it, Eva? Is my mother——'

'Mrs Stewart is quite herself again,' put in the nurse on

an impassive note. 'She'd like to see Miss Brentwood.'

Two or three hours ago such a summons might have given her hope, Toni thought. Right now all she could ask herself was where was the point? All Karen could want from her was the triumph of seeing her beaten. The last and greatest threat removed. If she had been content to sit back and wait, Rafe would probably have seen the light himself before it was too late.

'Toni?' Sean sounded uncertain. 'I thought that was what you wanted.'

'It was,' she said. She gave him a smile, coming to a sudden and philosophical decision. If satisfaction was what Karen wanted then why not let her have it? She had little enough of anything else. 'I'm on my way.'

Eva said nothing as they mounted the stairs together. Glancing at the plain features, Toni wondered fleetingly if the choice had been a deliberate one on Karen's part because of Rafe. Certainly a younger and prettier attendant might have provided a temptation.

'How long have you been with Mrs Stewart?' she heard herself asking.

'Three years,' came the reply.

'That's a long time.' She kept her tone light. 'I'd have thought you'd be living as one of the family by now.'

'I don't want to live as one of the family,' said Eva. 'When I'm not looking after Mrs Stewart I like my own company.'

'Does she really need a fulltime nurse?'

'Medically speaking, no. I'm more of a companion.' The smile that momentarily lit the other face revealed an hitherto unsuspected sense of humour. 'Not exactly what you'd expect in that department, am I, but we get along fine. I understand her, you see.'

They had reached the door at the end of the gallery. With her hand on the handle, Eva paused, her eyes skimming Toni's face to linger for a moment of naked but somehow moving envy on the pale gold fall of hair. 'There's something I ought to tell you before you go in there,' she said. 'I'll be leaving in a couple of months—family commitments. My father's going to need regular nursing by then, and I'm the obvious one to do it.'

'I'm sorry.' Toni meant that in more ways than the obvious, sensing the things left unsaid. This woman had given her life to the care of others, but that didn't signify any lack of regret for what might have been. She added softly, 'I'm afraid I shan't be here myself.'

'I know—she told me.' The hesitation was brief. 'You're wrong to go. She's been given in to a sight too much. Mr Stewart isn't doing her a kindness sending you away. She has to realise he's as much right to his freedom as she has to hers.'

'How?' Toni asked. 'Considering what happened this afternoon it hardly seems likely she's ever going to accept it.'

'She won't die of what happened this afternoon. If anything happens to Mr Rafe it might be a different story. She won't have anybody then.'

'She'll have Sean.'

'Who gives back only as much as he gets.' It was a simple statement of fact made without rancour. 'What she really needs is a whole family to fall back on—grandchildren to care about. If Sean marries at all it mightn't be for years, and I don't see him staying on here to comfort his mother—not without letting her see the sacrifice he's making at any rate. Rafe's another matter. He cares too much. That's the whole trouble.'

Toni's chest felt tight. 'Even if I agreed with you it wouldn't alter anything. He's the only one who can do anything about it, and he won't.'

'He isn't. You are. Maybe she only asked you to come up and see her because she wants to taunt you, but that wasn't the impression I got. I said she was herself again, but that was only so far as her physical state goes. Emotionally she's depressed where before she's been elated. Could be she's finally seeing things right. You'll know when you've talked to her.'

'Eva.' Toni put out a hand and touched the white sleeve as the woman made to open the door. Her voice had a catch in it. 'What makes you so sure I'm the right person?'

'Character judgement,' came the brief response. 'You'd do this whole family a lot of good.'

Toni doubted that. She had already done too much harm. Eva was well-meaning but in possession of too few facts. Rafe no longer wanted her to stay.

The room beyond the door was large and airy, furnished with just enough pieces to take away any bareness yet leave ample room for the passage of a wheelchair to any given point. Two doors led off it, one to either side. Eva made for the one on the left which already stood ajar, standing to one side to allow Toni prior access.

Karen lay propped in a high, narrow bed that had a pulley handle slung above it on a chain for her to lift herself upright. A console unit at the foot held a television and stereo tape deck, while to her hand was a control panel covering those and other functions, judging from the number of buttons set into it. Her wheelchair stood close by ready for use, the battery box at the rear making it look heavy and cumbersome when unoccupied.

'You can leave us alone, thank you, Eva,' she said. 'I'm quite comfortable.'

Toni remained where she was close by the door as the nurse went out again. There was something different about that face framed against the white pillows. It looked subtly older, the lines blurred. Karen had been weeping, she realised—not sobbing aloud, but deep down inside where it hurt the most.

'I'm sorry,' she said on impulse. 'I've caused you a lot

of trouble coming here. I don't have any excuses either. Pretending to be Sean's fiancée was inexcusable.'

'Yes, it was.' There was no accusation in the statement, just a stiff acknowledgement. 'Why did you agree to do it?'

There was little point in prevarication, Toni thought. It hardly mattered any more.

'To be with Rafe,' she said. 'Love makes fools of us all at times. In some ways you're as much to blame as I am. I'd never have fallen in love with him in the first place if you hadn't sent him to get me away from Sean.'

'Do you think I don't realise that?' Karen's tone was bleak. 'I didn't know then what you looked like—what you sounded like. Perhaps I should have guessed from Rafe's attitude when he spoke about you. He wasn't too reluctant to be persuaded to do as I asked. What I didn't bargain for was him falling in love with you.'

'He isn't in love with me,' Toni denied, feeling the hurt of that statement. 'Not the way you're talking about.'

It was a moment before Karen answered, her face registering confusion. 'He asked you to marry him,' she said at length. 'At least, he told me he was going to ask you.'

'He did, and I accepted. Only it wouldn't have lasted. He said as much tonight.'

'Then why did he do it?'

'To be honest, I think because you drove him to it. He needed a buffer, the way Sean thought he needed me.'

'Against me?'

Toni steeled herself to carry on. Eva knew this woman far better than anyone; she had to trust her judgement. 'Yes, against you. You saw no reason to let either of them be independent when you couldn't be yourself. Especially Rafe, because he made you the way you are. Isn't that right?'

'So what if it is?' came the sudden fierce demand. 'He made me a promise!'

'Which he's kept—which he'd still keep without the duress.'

'Providing another woman let him. Would you have done?'

'Yes, I would. Because I don't happen to believe in total possession. Rafe hasn't stayed with you out of duty; he's done it because he thinks enough of you to want to stay. He told me once that you were the most courageous person he knows because you'd never once let bitterness take over. I think he's wrong. You've never shown it, that's all.'

Karen's eyes were closed, her whole upper body trembling. When she spoke it was in little more than a whisper. 'Have you any idea what it's like to live like this? To see everything and everyone from the level of a bed or a chair? Rafe was in that car too, and he walked away.'

'And his father was killed.' Toni had moved to the bed, drawn there by compassion yet conscious still of the need to keep a sense of proportion. 'No, I can't imagine what it must be like. I don't think anyone could who hadn't experienced it for themselves. But however restricting, it has to be better than being dead. You have your eyes, your hearing, the use of your hands. Why don't you try using them to find some compensation? Take up painting, write a book. You could have talents you've never even thought about. And if you really want to count your lucky stars, think about those as handicapped as you who don't have all the aids and luxuries you probably take so much for granted.'

She stopped there, wondering if she had gone too far. Karen's eyes were open again, and she appeared to have been listening, but there was no telling her reactions. She looked frozen; immobile, her face as blank as an unwritten page.

Then suddenly that blankness was crumpling, her hand

coming out gropingly, reaching for Toni's swiftly extended one.

'Don't go,' she said thickly. 'I want you to stay.'

'I can't.' Toni made her voice as gentle as she could. 'Rafe doesn't want me to any more.'

'Because of me. Because I made it impossible. That won't happen again. Not now.'

'It's more than just that. He doesn't trust me. He doesn't really believe I never encouraged Craig Shannon.'

'That could be because you haven't been honest with him about other things.' She smiled faintly at the sudden tensing of the hand still holding hers. 'A man named Stevens, for instance. Randy Stevens.'

'How did you know?' It was Toni's turn to whisper, her mind racing to cope with the implications.

'Wheels within wheels.' Karen put pressure on the hand she now held. 'Sit down, Toni—on the bed. It doesn't matter.' She had gathered strength again. Only when Toni had nervelessly obeyed did she go on, tone rueful. 'You see, I had to have some fall back in case everything else failed, so I had a friend of a friend delve into your background via Immigration. They came up with the address you were staying at when you first arrived in the country—the same address as the man who went guarantor for you. I told Rafe, of course. He didn't seem surprised. He said you'd been reluctant to talk about your reasons for coming to Canada and now he could understand why.'

'He surmised I was living with Randy.' Toni put everything she knew into keeping her voice level. 'Is that it?'

'I guess we both did.' Karen paused, searching her face. 'Isn't that the way it was?'

'No.' She groped for words. 'I——'

'Save it for Rafe. He's the one entitled to hear it—if anyone is.'

'What's the use?' Toni asked on a dull note. 'He won't believe it. He probably won't even listen.'

'Then you'll have to make him listen. The way you made me listen a few minutes ago.' Her smile was wry. 'Nobody ever said the things you said to me before. They were overdue. If you stay you'd be good for me as well as Rafe. You could help me keep things in perspective.'

'*If* I stay.'

'I'd say there isn't much doubt. I knew the way things were with Rafe the moment I saw you two together for the first time. With the wicked stepmother out of the running he won't have a leg left to stand on either.'

'You're not wicked,' Toni responded, smiling with her. On impulse she leaned forward swiftly to press a kiss on the older woman's cheek. 'Given the opportunity, I think we could become the best of friends.'

'And if I have anything at all to do with it, we'll have it,' promised Karen. 'Why don't you go and find him right now? Tell him I want to see him.'

'He went riding.'

'Then we'll both have to wait.' She glanced up as a knock came on the door. 'This may be him now.'

It wasn't, it was Eva. 'If you're through talking, it's time you were having your bath,' she announced.

It was Toni who answered, getting up from the bed as she did so. 'We're through.'

'Only for the moment,' Karen stated with a certainty Toni wished she could share. 'Tomorrow's a whole new day.'

Outside on the gallery, Toni stood irresolute for a moment or two. If she went downstairs again there would be Sean to face with the inevitable questions, and she didn't think she could stomach that. She needed to be alone, to have time to think things through. Seeing Rafe again was going to be difficult enough after what he had said earlier. Telling him about Randy in a way he might understand seemed impossible.

It was cool and quiet in her room, the air-conditioning a soothing murmur.

Kicking off her shoes, she lay down on the bed with her hands supporting the back of her head and thought about nothing in particular, because forward planning was going to get her nowhere. If Rafe came at all it could only be to tell her it was no use. Asking her to marry him had been an impulse as swiftly regretted. He would not make the same mistake again.

The crash of thunder awoke her with a start, bringing her jerking upright on the bed. Although the blinds were down the next flash of lightning lit up the whole room, making her cower, despite herself. She had never been afraid of storms, but this one was right overhead and big enough to frighten anybody.

Her watch said ten o'clock. Rafe would not be coming now. If he had heard what his stepmother had to say he had obviously decided it made little difference in the long run. Knowing what he did know about Randy, Toni felt she could hardly blame him. From Randy to Craig to Sean and then to Rafe himself must seem like logical steps for a girl on the make to take. He might have blinded himself to that fact for a little while, but not any more. She would be going tomorrow as planned.

The rain sounded almost as loud as the thunder. She got up from the bed and went to the window to watch it, seeing the pool below turned to a seething, bubbling turmoil as lightning flashed yet again. Anyone out in that lot would have been soaked to the skin in seconds. One could only be thankful to be warm and snug indoors. With any luck it wouldn't last too long. Storms in these regions were usually over and done inside an hour, leaving the air cleansed and refreshed. In the meantime, there was nothing to do but wait. She had been doing a lot of that today.

The knock on her door came synonymously with the next clap of thunder, making her uncertain as to whether she had heard it or not. Only when it came again as the thunder rolled away into the distance did she slowly turn and walk across the room to open the door, looking at the man standing outside with an odd lack of emotion. He was wearing a dark silk dressing gown over matching pyjamas, his chest bare beneath the deep rolled collar. There was little to read from his expression. He could have been making a social call.

'I stayed out longer than I intended,' he said. 'It seemed pointless getting dressed again.' He paused there, still without change of expression. 'Karen said you had something to tell me.'

'Was that all she said?' Toni asked, and saw his mouth slant briefly.

'No, it wasn't all. I don't know how you managed it, but she wants you to stay on.'

'Do you?' Her voice was low. 'Or does that depend on what I have to tell you?'

'Maybe on the way you do tell it,' he came back. 'Do I get to come in, or do we conduct the whole conversation out here in the corridor?'

Gazing at that lean, inflexible face, Toni felt anger flower suddenly inside her, growing in seconds to unmanageable proportions. Why should she be expected to bare her soul unless he were prepared to do the same? If he didn't trust her now he was hardly going to take her word over anything she told him.

'We don't talk at all,' she said fiercely. 'I just changed my mind! I don't have to prove anything to you, Rafe. I'd rather never see you again than live with a man who can't trust his own judgement!'

He stopped the door from closing with a swift foot across the jamb, wincing as the hard edge cut into the leather slipper but keeping it there regardless to force his way through. Toni could only feel confusion as he pulled her to him, then his mouth found hers and she stopped thinking at all, conscious only of loving him and wanting him in a way which transcended all doubts.

Lying with her in his arms, minutes, hours, weeks later, he looked down into her face with a smile in his eyes. 'I'm sorry,' he said, 'I shouldn't have done that.'

'I'm glad you did,' she told him softly. 'I love you, Rafe.'

'It's mutual.' His own voice had a softness about it too. 'And it's permanent. No more suspicions. I'm willing to accept you might want me just for myself.'

'Such modesty,' she mocked, then sobered again to add on a wry note, 'I don't really mind telling you about Randy, you know.'

'Some other time,' he said. 'It stopped being important the moment you threw the whole thing in my teeth the way you did.' His voice roughened a little. 'I've been a fool. I could have lost you.'

'We could have lost each other,' she corrected. 'But we didn't, did we? We caught up in time.' She rubbed her cheek pleasurably against his chin, smiling as she did so. 'You've shaved again. Does that mean you planned this assault?'

'Maybe subconsciously I did. The only way I was sure of you was physically.'

'But not any more.'

'No,' he said, and there was no mistaking the look in his eyes. 'This time I'm sunk. Marry me soon, Toni.'

She held him close, thinking of all it was going to mean, of what she was taking on. Sean's future still needed straightening out, and Karen was not going to be easy to convince. Yet solutions could always be found if one tried hard enough, and with Rafe for a husband how could she fail?

'As soon as you like,' she said.

Harlequin Plus

BEAUTIFUL BANFF

Kay Thorpe could hardly have chosen a more romantic setting for her book than Banff, the picturesque resort town cradled on the eastern slopes of the snow-capped Canadian Rockies. Some of the most magnificent scenery in the world is here—crystal clear lakes nestling like turquoise jewels in the rugged mountainous landscape, bears, mountain goats, moose, caribou and wolves roaming free.

Each year some seven million visitors pass through the famous Banff National Park: in summer, to golf, canoe, camp, climb, explore and relax; and in winter, when heavy snowfalls turn Banff into one of the world's most spectacular winter playgrounds, to go cross-country and downhill skiing on the long and numerous trails.

The famous Banff Springs Hotel is a compelling sight in this magnificent setting. Built, enlarged, destroyed by fire and rebuilt in 1928, it looms romantically in Scottish-baronial-French-château splendor above the confluence of the Bow and Spray Rivers. Built on a grand, majestic scale, it complements the natural grandeur of its surroundings.

But even the finest photographer cannot capture on film the wonderful aroma of towering pine forests, the scent of breezes from the brilliant carpets of wild flowers, or the sparkling movement of tumbling mountains, streams and swift-flowing rivers. Truly breathtaking!

Harlequin
understands
Love...

and the way
you feel about it...

That's why women all over the world read

Harlequin Romances

Beautiful novels with that special blend
of Harlequin magic ... the thrill
of exotic places, the appeal of warmly
human characters, the tenderness
and sparkle of first love.

Enjoy six brand-new novels every month—
contemporary romances about women
like you ... for women like you!

Available at your favorite bookstore or through
Harlequin Reader Service

In the U.S.A.
1440 South Priest Drive
Tempe
AZ 85281

In Canada
649 Ontario Street
Stratford, Ontario
N5A 6W2